GRANTED BY THE BEAST

CONDUIT SERIES BOOK FOUR

REBECCA HAMILTON

CONNER KRESSLEY

EVER SCORCH

This book is dedicated to author April Canavan.
Without her support, this story wouldn't be possible.

CHAPTER 1

"ARE you sure this is where I'm supposed to be?" I shook my head and looked around at the darkened room where Ramsey had sent me for some ungodly reason. My only thought was that I should have brought a real flashlight. Oh, and maybe something to kill spiders with. Also, I hadn't gotten to eat dinner before I broke into this creepy building.

This place—an abandoned building in what had to be the most dangerous part of New York that even I had ever been to —smelled of urine and hopelessness. Although, I was used to that by now. I couldn't even remember how many twists and turns I had taken to get to the building that looked like it should have been torn down years ago.

It had been almost a year to the day since Ramsey and I had taken off to go on this crazy adventure. We'd been hunting down the darkness and dragging it into the light ever since *that* day. Sometimes, I hated the new job we'd taken on, and right about now was one of those times.

It had been a year since I had practically begged him to start teaching me how to hone and strengthen my powers. I still remembered the way he'd looked at me with pity when I'd done it.

A year since the worst pain of my life had made that necessary, and a year since I had felt anything close to whole. I didn't know if I'd ever be whole again, and that made all of this necessary. That made every single step I had taken into this dark and musty place extremely necessary.

Of course, I'm sure this is the right place, Ramsey said, speaking directly into my mind from the safety of his living room. I jumped a little as his words floated around me.

Though this mental connection we shared was nothing new, it still shook me a little every time. I had never been this close to anyone before, never let someone really dig around in my brain. Not again anyway. Not since I lost *him.*

All the magical readings point to the place you're standing right now, Ramsey continued. *Hell, there's enough energy bouncing off that place to light the entire city on fire. I'm surprised you can't feel it.*

"Well, I can't," I said, shrugging and looking out at the almost impenetrable darkness. "Tell me again, why aren't you here?"

The inside of this building was cold—much colder than it should have been, given the weather in the city right now. Still, old buildings were weird. They could get drafty. They could hold the cold like a ghost. I had learned that and more in my time living here before I went back to New Haven, before my life changed completely.

Maybe we should up our training sessions, Ramsey suggested, again directly into my head via the telepathic link. *Because, I have better things to do.*

No doubt one of those better things was to eat pizza and watch a movie while I did all the hard work. "We're already training five times a week," I balked. "I'm up at the crack of dawn every day. A girl's got to have some free time."

What went unsaid was the fact that I could only handle having so much magic in my life at any given time.

A girl also has to make sure she's safe, Ramsey countered. *Not that I'm speaking from experience or anything. But, if you're as intent as you seem on doing all of this by yourself, then I don't know what else to do but make sure you're as prepared for the unexpected as humanly possible.*

His voice cut out, and I knew what was coming next: the same mantra I had heard nearly every day for a year, the same warning that echoed through my head during my waking hours and haunted my dreams on the rare occasion that Abram didn't haunt them instead.

They're coming for you, Charisse. The Brothers are looking for you as we speak.

There it was, the ticking clock that had been planted firmly over my head. I hated it, but there was nothing I could do to erase it. That sound—the words that I could never forget—my life seemed to revolve around them, and I was tired of it.

"I know they're coming," I answered in a flat tone, and my words echoed off the walls around me. I swallowed hard at the thought of them. "Why do you think I'm doing this? You fight the small fries to work up to the big guys," I said, not really intending to rhyme. Still, I could think of worse results.

The Brothers aren't just big guys, Ramsey answered, the fearful tremble of his thought-voice rattling around in my skull. *They're two of the five Eternals. They were born in the fires that*—

"Created the universe. I know," I said, rubbing my arms as I stepped deeper into the creepy dwelling. *Satina gave me the rundown before she died. I know what The Brothers are.*

As I brought up the Supplicant's name, my entire body shuddered. That woman, who I thought hated me when we first met, became something of a friend to me before her untimely passing. In fact, she became something of a best friend. Now that she was gone, she was more of a martyr figure, and the truth of that shook me to my core.

What Satina told you was a sliver of the truth, the same way a history teacher might tell her students that Hitler was 'sort of a bad guy.'

"Sounds like a lackluster history teacher," I mumbled under my breath.

I traced my hand along the stone wall covered in dust, ash, and something I couldn't quite place. Whatever I was supposed to find here, I wasn't finding it. All I could see was hard lines and shadows, abandoned wooden tables, stone walls, and a cracked, oil-stained concrete floor.

I couldn't sense any of the power that Ramsey said was here, and it was starting to make me mad. I'd spent the entire last year training and improving my skills, and yet he could sense magic in a building where I was getting nothing.

I wanted to reach out and punch something in my frustration, but I didn't want Ramsey to know how affected I was by all of this.

As my vision adjusted to the darkness, I could just barely make out the caged lights overhead. Without working electricity, they wouldn't do me any good.

A magical signature of some kind should be calling to me like a beacon, but nope, nothing. Even as I felt around on tables in the muted light, I found little more than broken pieces of plaster and drywall, a hammer, and a paint can that had been tipped over.

My foot caught on a crack in the concrete floor, and I stumbled forward, catching myself on an old wooden chair before I could hit the ground. I growled under my breath, and listened to it echo off the walls around me.

Even something malevolent would have made an appearance, especially if it was looking for a weakness before making itself known. I hadn't made a mistake like that in months, and here I was, acting like a scared little girl again.

"There's nothing here, Ramsey." What I didn't say was that if he hadn't wasted my time, I might be able to do something that was *actually* useful.

If I stayed much longer, I might find some cobwebs and maybe even a rats nest or two, but I doubted even the spiders and vermins still lived here. Everything about this place felt dead and abandoned. It made my skin crawl.

Be that as it may, the truth is The Brothers are a threat unlike any the world has ever seen before. You know that. That's why— Ramsey gasped, and my head whipped around. *What was that?*

I froze, listening as hard as I could into the silence. "What was what?"

I couldn't hear anything, and he was starting to act like a crazy person.

Don't tell me you didn't hear that, he said, and I could feel the tension filling the air like that time last month when he'd walked into the bathroom while I was changing. I fought the urge to giggle at the memory of me beating him upside the head with a towel rack.

I shook it off and got back into fight mode. "It's kind of hard to hear with you blabbering on in my head." My muscles tensed, and my magic flared up in reaction to whatever had Ramsey on edge. "Also, are you using my ears again? You know I hate it when you do that."

I figured one of us had better make use of them.

"Very funny," I muttered before I took a step forward and through the doorway. "What did you hear?" I still couldn't hear anything, and I was being as quiet as I could, which was pretty quiet after all my practice.

It was a low sound, he answered. *Kind of like a whistling.*

I fought the urge to roll my eyes, again. "You think there's an open window?" I asked, looking around for any indication that there was an open window anywhere, let alone any window period..

I tried to avoid using magic unless necessary. Although I was a self-energizing never-ending source of magic, I still hadn't figured out how to manipulate and use my magic without burning out completely. I needed to save my efforts for the right moments.

This was turning into one of those moments I was worried

about. If something or someone was here, I needed to know about it, and the sooner the better.

I extended my hand and visualized a golden ball of light materializing in my hand, even though I would have preferred to use a flashlight. The only problem was that my phone had inexplicably died the moment I walked into the building. Being both Supplicant and Conduit, I could conjure magic, and I could do it using my own blood as an energy source. This ball of light would illuminate the room; at least, that was the plan.

Only problem was, when I called forth my magic, nothing happened. Like absolutely nothing. It felt like I was back in New Haven, helpless to stop what was happening to me.

"What the hell?" I murmured aloud. "My powers aren't working."

What? Ramsey asked, as though he didn't believe what I'd just said. *Are you sure you're doing it the right way?*

Just like that, I was thrust back into our first lesson, where he'd called everything I had ever done with my powers into question.

"It's an illumination spell, Ramsey," I said to the mage, trying to resist the urge to roll my eyes. "I could do that in my sleep. Hell, I have done it in my sleep, and more than a few times at that."

Hold on a second.

It sounded as though Ramsey was shuffling around in the brownstone we called both our home and base of operations back in the city. I could hear him stuff the rest of his food in his mouth, and I wanted to punch him for eating it when I couldn't have any. He knew pizza was my favorite.

I took another step forward, hesitating when I couldn't really see what was going on in front of me.. "What is it we're looking for in here again?" I couldn't remember Ramsey ever telling me exactly what it was that I was searching for. "It better not be something stupid."

As I moved, I finally began to feel the energy that Ramsey was talking about. With it pulsing and coursing over my skin now, I could see why he was so surprised I couldn't feel it before. How was it he put it again? Enough energy bouncing off this place to light the entire city on fire?

I hadn't felt it then, but within moments of trying to use my own magic, the unseen energy hit me so hard it shook me, yanking me forward without my consent.

Ramsey!" I said, my heart skipping a beat. What had he gotten me into?

An artifact, he answered. *A hidden treasure of immense power. That's all I know.*

"Screw this," I said. "Something's pulling me, Ramsey."

I focused my energy on retreating from the force that had been pulling me forward into the darkness.

What? he asked. *Charisse, is it cold in there? Colder than it has any right to be?*

I huffed a breath out, and when I could see it, I knew. "Yep."

Run, Charisse! he said quickly. *Get the hell out of there!*

Not that I really needed him to tell me, because I already wanted to get out of there as soon as possible.

Ramsey, what am I dealing with? I asked, feeling terror through the telepathic connection between us.

A nightmare, he said. *A Shadow Elf. It's a nasty thing that turns itself into your worst nightmare. You're not ready for it. You'll never survive on your own. Get the hell out of there. Now!*

I spun and headed toward the open door, only to have it slam shut in my face. Freaking magic. Always popping up when I least expected it.

"Ramsey," I said, grabbing the handle and finding it not budging. I was trapped. "Ramsey, I don't think getting out of here is gonna be possible."

I turned around, trying to find another way to escape, another way to get away.

Static filled my head, cutting off the connection between me and the mage that had been my partner for an entire year. Just as quickly as it started, the noise in my head shifted from mildly uncomfortable into a pain so unbearable that I fell to the floor, clutching my head to soften the feedback.

It wasn't long until all of it faded completely, leaving my connection to Ramsey broken as well as a headache that I wasn't sure would ever go away.

"Charisse," a soft voice said, breaking through the silence in my mind. It took me a second to figure out why it was different. Then, I realized it wasn't coming from my head, but from inside the building. "I've been waiting for you."

Looking up, I did my best not to shriek in surprise at what I saw. My heart was still racing from the unexpected pain a few moments before, and I was attempting to force myself to calm down.

I blinked rapidly, willing the hallucination to vanish, but it didn't. Standing there was my best friend Lulu with a tray of cookies in her hands. She held it out to me with a smile.

"Well," I muttered as I reached out to take a cookie. "This is an unexpected surprise."

CHAPTER 2

LULU WAS my best friend in the entire world. She had been for as long as I could remember. I didn't have a sister. Hell, I didn't have a family at all anymore. If I had, though, Lulu would have been it. She was the person I thought about when I needed support, especially with Abram gone. She was the shoulder I could lean on, and her children were most likely the closest thing I'd ever get to having my own.

So, seeing her here was almost the opposite of scary. It was actually comforting. What was up with that? Especially since I knew that there was no way she would be there without her two children close by. And there was no way in hell that she'd bring her kids into an abandoned building like this one.

"Ramsey," I said while I ate a cookie and stared at the visage of a woman I loved holding her special homemade cookies. "What the hell is this about?" '

Her being some sort of magical apparition didn't change the fact that I was starving.

There was no answer.

"Ramsey," I repeated, starting to get a little worried. After all, even if this thing—this Shadow Elf—had missed the mark completely while trying to scare me, I was still trapped in an abandoned building on the bad side of town with something that was capable of mimicking my best friend's appearance.

Life could certainly be better.

"He isn't in there anymore, Charisse," said the thing that looked like Lulu, a smile draping across her perfectly made-up face. "It was so crowded, and I wanted some privacy. We need to talk, just us girls."

The tittering coming from the monster wearing my best friend's skin was extremely creepy.

"You're not my friend," I said, my hands balling into fists and my eyes narrowing. "Although, the resemblance is striking."

Which was to say, she looked like a skinny version of myself—dark hair, light eyes, but sans the eye freckle I'd inherited from my father. Oh, and the two minions that she never went anywhere without.

Shadow-Lulu shook her head. "Mages aren't always right, you know," she said. "I could be your friend. I could have been hiding some deep dark truth about my personal identity all these years. Lord knows, I wouldn't have been the only one. But let's say your little mage was right. Let's say I am the thing he thinks I am. Would that make me so bad?" Her voice was honeyed, and I remembered the last time I saw Lulu in reality.

"I'm gonna go out on a limb here and say...yes."

The shadow-thing standing in front of me had no idea how things had ended with Lulu and myself. It obviously had no clue that I'd actually killed Lulu's brother, and that she probably wouldn't be standing in front of me with a tray of cookies if she ever found out.

It was time to get up completely, and I did it without taking my eyes off the Shadow Elf. I took a deep breath and centered myself. That was the thing about me, though. I wasn't the same girl I had been even a year ago. I was different. Harder. Stronger. Losing the person you loved could do that to a girl. So if this Shadow Elf was intent on scaring me, it was going to have its work cut out for it. Especially if it was going to use my best friend's skin to do it.

"Don't you find that way of thinking to be a little narrow-minded?" she asked, holding the tray of cookies up higher as if to offer them to me again. "After all, just because I am what I am, it doesn't make me a bad person."

"It doesn't make you a person at all," I clarified and glanced over my shoulder at the shut door. "But if it did, I would say that the fact you're holding me captive in this building makes you a bad person more than anything else." I shook my head. "And you can keep the damn cookies. To be honest with you, they don't taste a thing like the real you would make. You're obviously missing the secret ingredient."

Shadow-Lulu chuckled bitterly, dropping the cookies and all sense of pretense along with it. The tray slammed hard against the floor, clattering and spilling cookies everywhere as it did. Then, the cookies disappeared as though they had never been there in the first place.

Shame. The cookies were the best thing Shadow-Lulu had going for it. Plus, I was still hungry.

"As if anyone could trap the legendary Charisse Bellamy," she said. "It would be easier to draw blood from a stone. At least, that's the word on the street." Shadow-Lulu looked around like she couldn't believe her luck, and that's when I knew something was up.

I tilted my head to the side. "And what street would that be exactly?"

"The only one that matters, of course," she answered. "The street of wonder."

Okay. So this Shadow Elf was going to hit me with a lot of fortune cookie bullshit that didn't really mean anything. I didn't have time for this. I was losing my patience.

"You should tell the people on that street that *you* did it, then," I said, stepping forward. "I'm sure they'd be very impressed."

"Not nearly as impressed as they are by you," said the thing wearing Lulu's face with a smirk that looked like it belonged on a demented clown.

It was weird, hearing all this crap come at me with the voice of my best friend. I had always been close to Lulu. It wasn't like our friendship had ever been contentious. I wasn't used to that sweet, good-natured voice being this combative with me. Well, except for the one time that I almost lost her son. That had been an accident, though.

Still, if this Shadow Elf thought this was all it was going to take to break me, then it didn't know me very well, regardless of whether it could get into my head or not.

If this thing wanted to waste all its time spouting off some nonsense about an imaginary road just to make a metaphorical point, then I was more than happy to do that. After all, this sort of stalling only served to allow me to pool my powers enough to come at this thing with the kind of blast that would knock an elephant on its ass, let alone something that looked like a one-hundred-and-ten-pound woman.

Lulu had always been the tiny one in our friend circle, and I could only hope that the Shadow Elf taking on her form would work in my favor for that reason. But the truth was, I had no idea how any of this would work. Looks could be deceiving in more ways than one. Plus, my magic hadn't been reliable since I entered the decrepit building.

"You're selling yourself short, Charisse Bellamy," the Shadow Elf said. She shook her head and pursed her lips at me. It was a face I'd never seen Lulu make herself, and the off-look only helped me to separate the illusion from the monster. "Would The Brothers really be so interested in someone who wasn't impressive? Something tells me that you're worth every bit of fuss that's come at you."

I startled a little. This thing knew about The Brothers? Maybe there was something to all of this after all.

That was when common sense caught up with me. *Of*

course it knew about The Brothers. It was in my head, and given that The Brothers were immortal, super powerful beings who were seemingly hellbent on my destruction, they naturally took up a lot of my headspace.

While I kept pooling my power, I knew that I needed to let Shadow-Lulu keep talking. Once I had enough that I was sure I could not only take this thing out but bust a hole into the building I now found myself trapped in, I'd take action. Judging by the way I could feel the magic building, it would only be a few more seconds. Until then, I just needed to keep this thing talking.

"You're going to have to go deeper into my psyche than that if you want to scare me," I said, still letting the energy inside of me form a base in my gut.

"How much deeper would you like me to go?"asked the thing that looked like Lulu, tilting her head to the side. "Should I go to the part of your brain that is, at this moment, actively trying to destroy me? Or would you prefer that I went deeper still? Would you prefer that I ventured into the broken part? The part not even your mage knows about? I took this guise out of respect to you, to show you that I wasn't here to fight. I can take another if you'd like. I can take the one that would hurt you the most. The one that would decimate you."

The air seemed to shift and, as it did, Lulu morphed in front of me. She grew taller, broader. Her light hair was replaced with dark, and her face twisted into the face I wanted to see more than any other in my life. The face that haunted every single one of my nightmares.

"Abram," I muttered before I could stop myself.

I knew it wasn't him. I knew the man I loved was gone forever, that he was never coming back. Still, the sight of him was enough to pull all the air out of the room. It was enough to break through my defense and rip apart the concentration that I was using to mount an offense. Just the sight of him.

That was all it took. It didn't matter that he wasn't really there, that I hadn't seen him in a year.

"I could be," the Shadow Elf said. "You see, we get a bad reputation, us Shadow Elves, but the truth is we can be anything you'd like. We don't have to focus on your fears." The thing that looked like Abram walked toward me, biting his lower lip and grinning at me in a way that sent me back into the sweetest moments of my life, the ones where he held me through the night. As he neared me, the sensations got even stronger. It was insane. This thing even smelled like Abram, his musty sweet scent filling me and lighting me up inside. "We can also be your fantasy," he said, reaching out to brush his fingers across my face.

I wanted more than anything to let him, to fall into the lie that the man standing before me right now actually was the love of my life. I wanted to believe that the last year hadn't happened, and that every bit of heartache I'd experienced was nothing more than a fever dream. I wanted it to be something I could shrug off as I went on with building the life I wanted with the man I thought I'd have forever with.

I couldn't, though. I wasn't the type of woman who could lie to herself anymore. I wasn't the sort of person who could allow herself to be deceived, even by her own will. Maybe once upon a time I could have done that, but I wasn't that little girl anymore.

I froze under his hand, a shudder of ice-cold energy run through me. My body stiffened, my face tightened, and my soul steeled over. What was happening here wasn't a fantasy. It was a mockery, and I'd be damned if I was going to let the love of my life be picked apart and manipulated by something that didn't deserve to lick the soles of his boots.

"Touch me again, and it'll be the last thing you ever do," I growled, tossing the thing's hand aside and staring daggers into its face. "You don't want to frighten me? Fine. That's smart. I'm a big girl. You probably couldn't anyway, if we're being honest." I lifted my hand and let a bit of the energy I had been storing come out, crackling along my fingertips and sending loud pops through the air. "Something's got *you* scared, though. Right? That's why you're here. That's why you were waiting for me. It's why you want me. You want me to drive a stake in whatever creature is out there keeping the monsters up at night. Am I right?"

The thing that looked like Abram took a deep breath. Unblinking, it answered, "You don't understand. If it gets out, then it'll mean hell for all of us. This isn't some run-of-the-mill demon. Even the Brothers couldn't handle it. Why do you think—"

"Shut up." I thrust my hand toward the thing. It scuttled backward, folding in a way the real Abram never would. "Stop wearing his face," I commanded. "You don't deserve it."

Again, the air shifted, and Abram's body changed. In seconds, I was no longer looking at the man I loved. Hell, I wasn't even looking at a man. The thing that stood before me was a living shadow. It had eyes and teeth, but nothing else of merit. It was a blob of darkness floating in front of me that didn't have a body.

"My God," I muttered without thinking.

"You're not exactly my type, either," the Shadow Elf snapped, darting about in the air. "But that's beside the point. You were brought here because of a magic powerful enough to send ripples through the entire city in a way that no one could control. That was real. It wasn't anything I made up. I knew you would come for it. Given all the work you and that mage have done to keep this place safe, I figured, sooner or later, you'd find your way here. Once you did, I'd convince you to kill him. I didn't expect you to be so hard-headed or unwilling to do the right thing."

"I get that a lot," I admitted, my voice still a stern thing. "And I don't kill anything that doesn't deserve it. So, if you—"

15

"You won't want to," the Shadow Elf said. "You'll think you have a choice, but there is no choice. There's nothing that can be done. It's too powerful. It's too much, and he has to die before this thing gets out of hand."

"Don't tell me what to do," I snapped. "Now, unless you want me to turn you into a dark puddle on the floor, I suggest you turn the lights back on and let me see exactly what it is you want me to kill so badly."

"Charisse," the Shadow Elf said quickly. "It's not what it looks like. If you'd just—"

"Now!" I commanded, the power around my hands sparking even more.

The Shadow Elf grimaced, turning into a blob of darkness in front of me, all teeth and eyes.

But the lights in the building came on, revealing a man on the floor, tied up and unconscious. The man the Shadow Elf had been telling me needed to die.

And he was no stranger at all.

In fact, I knew him quite well.

"Jesus," I muttered, rushing toward him. "My God." My eyes went wide as I looked at the Shadow Elf, anger rushing up in me like a wave. "What the hell have you done to Huntsman?"

CHAPTER 3

"CHARISSE!" yelled the Shadow Elf behind me in a disgusting display of desperation. "You don't understand!"

Flipping around, I thrust a fist toward him. My anger rushed out of me in the form of a blast of golden energy. It slammed against the shadow thing, sizzling as it sent him spiraling back toward the wall. There was a part of me that yelled for caution, but my friend was chained up like an animal, and I needed to do something. *Now.*

The creature hit the wall hard, screaming as it slid down and rested on the scarred concrete floor. As I turned back to Huntsman, it occurred to me I had threatened to turn that thing into a dark puddle on the floor, and that was exactly what I had just done. It wouldn't be enough to kill it, but it would keep it at bay for a while, and it definitely hurt like hell.

"Cha-Charisse," the Shadow Elf said from its place on the floor. I was surprised it was still able to speak, that it was still conscious, or whatever passed as conscious for a shadow.

"Shut the hell up, monster!" I said, leaning down beside Huntsman to examine his wounds.

His long dark hair splayed against the concrete, a bruise marred his cheek, and blood matted along his hairline by his left temple. Even beaten and broken, Huntsman was a handsome man with his Roman nose, square jaw, and hulking, muscular form.

But not as handsome as Abram.

My heart panged at the memory, and I had to push the distraction away. It was hard, though. Abram was always there. Always taking his place in my heart and mind that I couldn't erase. Every step I took, even though it took me further away from him, he was there by my side. But I didn't have time for Abram. Not now. My friend needed help, and I needed to find a way to help him.

I placed my ear against Huntsman's chest, listening for the heartbeat that would tell me if he was still alive. When I heard the telltale signs of life, I almost cried in relief. His breaths were coming slow and soft, his heartbeat faint, but he was still alive.

My guess was this thing *couldn't* kill him, which was why it was trying to get me to do it. Just the same, I needed to get my friend out of here, because being trapped like this was nearly as bad as being dead anyway.

I reached for the ropes tying Huntsman's hands and feet, hoping I might be able to loosen the knots, but when my fingers grazed the twisted fibers, red energy snapped at me, sending me flying backward on my ass.

"Damn it!" I yelled, making a fist and then almost collapsing from the pain. The ropes had seared right through my fingertips with their magic. "What did you do? What kind of spell is holding those ropes?"

I expected the Shadow Elf to reply to me, maybe offer a weak verbal sparring or try to give me information that had nothing to do with what was holding Huntsman here. I expected the Shadow Elf to try and manipulate me. I was prepared, too.

Instead, a much more familiar and soothing voice entered

my head and pulled me out of the murderous rage that had taken over my body.

Charisse, are you okay? Ramsey asked, more than a little concern tracing his voice as it trickled through my mind.

"Ramsey?" I swallowed hard and rubbed my fingertips against the inside of my palms, trying to make them feel better. "I'm okay. I'm fine. The Shadow Elf tried to screw with my head, but I put him on his ass."

The Shadow Elf, still a shapeless orb on the floor, spoke. "I'm just trying to make you see what's happening. I didn't mean you any harm."

Ramsey hissed. *Luring you into an abandoned building with the illusion of a magical imprint of an artifact and then cutting you off from the outside world is a weird way of showing that.*

Because our connection had been reestablished, he could hear what I heard and see what I saw. The Elf couldn't hear Ramsey, though. Not that it mattered. We had much more pressing issues to deal with.

Is that Huntsman? Ramsey asked as I turned back to the man on the floor.

"It is." I stepped closer so Ramsey could get a better sight through my eyes of Huntsman's current condition. "The Shadow Elf tried to convince me to kill him. He's got him tied up with ropes that have been spelled or something. I can't get them off."

I'll deal with it, Ramsey said. *You're not by the door, are you?*

"No," I said, narrowing my eyes. "Why?"

Because I'm coming in, he called through my mind. *And I'm doing it the hard way.*

As the words left his mouth, a loud banging reverberated through the room. The metal door under the glowing red exit sign flung open, and on the other side of it, Ramsey stood with a pistol in his hand. The damn thing was basically smoking as he stepped through, allowing the door to clang shut behind him.

Ramsey wasn't a powerful man. Not in size, stature, *or* magical ability. He couldn't even kill someone, thanks to the limit on abilities bestowed to mages that prevented them from using their magic to take a life. Still, he was the best friend I had these days, and he served as a steadying and wise presence in my life. Having him in my head meant the world, but having him by my side meant even more. Especially when I was up against something I'd never encountered before.

"You're here?" I asked, standing as a rush of relief ran through me. He was a welcome sight, to say the least.

"Of course I'm here," Ramsey said, holstering his firearm that was really only any good for show, or, well, blowing down doors apparently. "I couldn't hear you anymore. I wasn't about to sit there while you dealt with the fight of your life. I had to come. Even if it was just to pick up the pieces of whoever you blew apart." He winked at me and then turned to face the Shadow Elf.

Warmth ran through me as I nodded at the man who had come to be as much of a friend as I had ever had in the year I had spent without Abram. He was a shoulder for me to cry on, and a mentor for me to learn from, even if we weren't of quite the same species.

There was something decidedly Sherlock Holmes-like about the man, which often made me wonder what Briar saw in him. Not that he wasn't handsome, but Briar had always been more the type to date jocks. Or, well, whoever I was dating at the time. That was water at the end of the runway now, and ever since the events on Grimoult Island, we were all friends.

The Shadow Elf eyed Ramsey from the floor. "You shouldn't have come," he said. His voice sounded stronger now, more potent and capable. "If Charisse Bellamy will not do as I ask, then I must do more to inspire her. I will give you ten seconds to leave here, mage. Her stubbornness has sealed her fate. It would be a shame to see you die alongside her."

Ramsey looked at me through his rectangular wire-framed glasses, neither breaking stride nor looking at the shadow creature as it spoke.

"He's got a big mouth, doesn't he?" he asked, coming up to greet me.

I rolled my eyes. "You have no idea."

"I don't need ten seconds, my man," Ramsey said, settling beside me and pushing me with his shoulder. "This girl and me, we're kind of ride or die."

"Die it is, then," the Shadow Elf said.

With that, the lights went out and left us once again in the dark.

Ramsey wrapped his hand around my own, and I could tell immediately that the mental connection between us had been blocked again, probably by the Shadow Elf and its magic. We were going to have to talk to each other by more natural means, which meant there would be no advantage of keeping our planned actions a secret from our attacker.

With his hand still in mine, Ramsey pressed his back against mine in a standard move meant to ensure that, between the two of us, we'd be able to see things coming and not be caught by surprise. Or, at least, see the shadows of things coming at us. I couldn't see anything clearly in the darkness. We'd been practicing this for a year, though, and shadows would do just fine.

"Why does he want Huntsman dead?" Ramsey asked over my shoulder.

"Says he's too powerful." I narrowed my eyes, as if that might help me see through the darkness.

Lifting my hand, I cast a silent spell meant to turn my fist into a beacon of light that we could use to see with. The spell worked, causing bright light to burst forth from me. But somehow, it did nothing to illuminate the warehouse around us. We were still stuck in darkness.

"That doesn't make sense," Ramsey said. "Huntsman's a

damn good warrior, and that axe of his is impressive, but I wouldn't call him powerful enough to set Shadow Elves on edge." His hand tightened around mine. "And that won't work. This isn't regular darkness. It's part of his spell. The isolation is only needed for the more personal illusions."

"Good thing we're not isolated, then," I said, nodding firmly. "I've got you. A little darkness never scared me."

"You won't have him for long," the Shadow Elf said from somewhere in the darkness, using a voice that sounded every bit as ominous as he looked in his natural form. Or her. I still didn't know what it claimed as a gender.

Just then, a tug pulled hard at my hand. I thought it was Ramsey at first, but I wasn't being pulled toward him. I was being jerked away.

"What the hell?" I tightened my grip on my partner's hand. I'd already lost the love of my life. I wasn't about to let anyone take someone else I cared about away from me.

"He's trying to separate us," Ramsey said, panic filling his voice. "If he does that, we won't stand a chance. We won't be able to tell the difference between what's real and what's fake."

"I knew the difference," I said as the force pulled my friend away from me again. I wasn't trying to be cocky, but it was the truth.

Once more, I latched onto Ramsey, though this time I only managed to get his hand with the tips of my fingers. His hands were clammy and mine were sweating. I could feel him slipping away, no matter how hard I held onto him.

"If you knew the difference, it was because he wanted you to know the difference," Ramsey said defiantly, snorting at the end for good measure. "He wanted to convince you it was in your best interest to kill Huntsman. Since you're not going to—"

The energy pulled at me again. This time, I couldn't fight

it. Ramsey's hand slipped away, and I was left alone. I screamed as I lost him, but the scream was short-lived.

When the lights flickered back on, Ramsey was floating in the air. He was frantically throwing his arms around as though he was swimming. His mouth was closed, and his cheeks were filled, as though he was holding his breath and trying to ge. The Shadow Elf floated beside him.

"Do you want to know the most dangerous thing about fear, Charisse?" the Shadow Elf asked, bobbing around in the air, the warehouse rafters an uneasy backdrop behind his smokey black head.

I felt something at its words. Something harsh and dangerous crossing through my mind. I kept my mouth shut, though. The most important thing I could do would be to listen and absorb everything the Shadow Elf had to say.

"Fear's powerful enough to actually kill you."

"You're wrong," I couldn't help telling him.

"Defiant, as always. Even in your dreams, my dear. You're stubborn and bullheaded. But you're not the same girl that you were when you first started this journey," the Shadow Elf said. "The Charisse that first discovered the magic in our world, she would have run screaming from the situation that you're in. You know the choice you have to make, girl. You're going to have to pick one or the other. You're stronger now than you've ever been before, and you're strong enough to make the right choice."

The Shadow Elf was trying to be soothing, I could tell. That didn't change the fact that I wanted to punch him in the face.

"I don't have to make a choice for you," I shouted. The Shadow Elf was right, though. I wasn't the same girl that had started this journey. I had power, and it was time that I showed it. "You're a monster, and if you hurt either one of them, I won't do a single thing for you. In fact, I'm sure that I can find a way to end your miserable existence."

A dark chuckling brought me up short, and the defiance and confidence that I'd felt only moments before quickly faded into reluctant fear. My hands were sweating, but the Shadow Elf didn't need to know that. It didn't need to know that I was afraid, but something about the way it was staring at me told me that my fear didn't go unnoticed.

"Your mage here is afraid of dark water. Since he was a child, he's always been afraid he would meet his end struggling for air in the freezing depths of the ocean." The creature's teeth spread into a horrific smile. "Now, he believes he is, and that belief is enough to help end his life. You will kill the Huntsman. You'll do it right now, or you'll be forced to watch your mage here suffocate before your very eyes."

I had a decision to make, and I wasn't sure that I could do it. I looked over at where Huntsman lay unconscious on the floor. He saved my life in Grimoult, when we were faced against almost impossible odds. Then, I turned to look at Ramsey who was suffocating on air. He'd been the only person I could trust since the day I lost Abram.

How was I supposed to choose between them?

My eyes darted between the two men who meant as much to me as they possible could, and I knew the choice was impossible.

"Be quick, Charisse Bellamy," the Shadow Elf said. "It doesn't look like Ramsey has much time, and the clock is ticking."

CHAPTER 4

My MIND RACED as I took stock of what was happening in front of me. Stupid Ramsey. If he'd have just stayed where he was, if only he wouldn't have gone racing through town to make sure I was safe, then this wouldn't be happening.

I couldn't let Ramsey die. Not after everything he'd done for me.

Still, I wasn't about to kill Huntsman just to stop it from happening. I wasn't a murderer, and besides, Ramsey wasn't the only man in this room who had been there for me. Huntsman had saved my life as well. He was a hero, and if this shadow monster thought Huntsman was powerful enough that he needed to be dead, then that told me everything I needed to know.

"I will destroy you," I said, keeping my voice as calm and serious as possible. "Make no mistake. If you do this, I'll kill you. I'll scatter your molecules so far across the vast reaches of space that they'll never come back together."

The Shadow Elf laughed again, the unnerving tone sending cold shivers along my spine.

"Do you think I fear death, Charisse Bellamy?" He turned his head as Ramsey struggled to breathe in the invisible bubble that was slowly drowning him. "When faced with what's to come, death would be a welcome respite. I do what I do for this world, for the people I care about. I do what I do for you, even if you refuse to see it."

And that was it. As sure as I was standing here, that thing had just showed me it's Achilles' Heel. It cared about something, which meant it had something to lose. I knew more than most that having something to lose made you weak.

For just a second, Abram's face flashed in my mind, and I had to force it away.

Energy crackled around my hands as I crafted a silent but complicated spell. It was the same spell I'd used on Ramsey during our last training session. The same one that left him debilitated for hours, unable to move for fear of the pain it would bring his body.

Even as I cast the spell, I couldn't help but smile at what I knew was going to happen to the Shadow Elf. If it was anything similar to what had happened to Ramsey, it would throw the monster across the room and practically tear it to pieces.

Thrusting my hands forward, I shot a ball of energy at the shadow thing. The creature flinched as my magic collided with it...

...but nothing else happened.

There was no big reaction. There was no flying across the room. The elf didn't even flinch as the energy sparked around his skin, seeming to sink into his flesh one layer at a time. Soon, all of the energy I had directed at him dissipated, and he was there with that same ridiculous smile on his face.

"Looks like you're already losing your juice," the Shadow Elf said, glee pouring out of him like water from an open faucet.

"Not necessarily," I said, feeling the connection between us set itself up as the magic I'd just pummeled the monster with took effect. "My powers aren't weakening, you sadistic bastard."

What I hadn't even thought about before I cast the spell was what had happened to Ramsey *after* I did it. That's what I was waiting for. So, while I waited for him to realize what I'd done, I returned the creature's smile.

If a mass of black energy could make a facial expression, then the Shadow Elf's eyebrows were pulling together, perhaps feeling from the inside the sensation of my magic curling around his insides and taking root.

"It's spreading," I said, hoping he felt every bit of fear as I did in that moment. I wanted to remind him that I wasn't the only one who might lose here. Plus, there was that little bit of New York in me that demanded that if I went down, I took him down with me.

"What?" the Shadow Elf asked, and though I couldn't tell for sure that his eyes had widened, the lilt in his voice spoke to intense confusion.

No, more than confusion.

Acceptance of the inevitable.

He knew what was going on. He could feel the tendrils of my magic seeping into him and refusing to let go. He could sense my magical fingers wrapping themselves around his nonexistent windpipe and squeezing tightly. He knew what I had done, and he knew just how effective it was going to be. Especially because he could now see directly into my mind and the spell I'd cast.

The blob of darkness began to twist. "You bitch!"

Around me, visions played like hologragrams of my real life. My real past. Every moment that had ever pained me, brought into reality. Excruciating detail showed me exactly what my worst memories were.

My father walking out, never to return.

My mother dying of cancer.

Abram.

Each scene beckoned me, pulling me in three directions all at once. Although I knew it was a facade, the compulsion was still there to run to them, to try and keep the inevitable from happening in a way that would tear apart my existence.

The Shadow Elf was playing dirty, there was no doubt about it. But I knew the one way to fight back against darkness. Hell, I'd spent the last year doing exactly that.

I blasted more of my light at the creature, taking the pain of each milieu he'd presented me and focusing it into the energy I pushed outward. That's right. I turned every memory that he was forcing me to relive into a weapon that I could use against him. I smiled again. This time it was at the strength that I had, and the power that I now carried. There was no way in hell that the creature in front of me stood a chance. Not when I wasn't the same girl he figured I was.

The creatures I went up against really did underestimate me, and I was definitely getting tired of it. That didn't stop me from what came next.

All my pain, all my grief, came rushing out of me in the form of white and gold sparks. My magic stabbed into the Shadow Elf like a thousand tiny needles, this time absorbing into his skin nearly the instant it touched.

The painful vision he'd projected flickered out of existence, replaced with the knowledge that I'd already lived through them and I could face anything that was thrown at me. The Shadow Elf writhed back and forth, growling out more words, this time unintelligible, until finally he cemented into one solid form.

Abram. Again.

My energy hadn't defeated it. Instead, my pain had told it all it needed to know. Of all the hurt in my life, it'd determined losing Abram was my greatest. Now, it was going to try and play off that weakness.

The Shadow Elf threw his arms—Abram's arms—out to

his sides. "You need to stay away from me," he said. "For good."

Just like before, it was a stab directly through my heart and into my soul.

It was one of the last things Abram had said to me. Like the moment was replaying from my mind. I knew what he was doing, what he was trying to accomplish. That didn't take away the pain, though.

"Don't come looking for me. And promise me one other thing." The Shadow Elf, in Abram's form, blinked hard. "Have a good life."

What was this creature playing at? I knew it wasn't Abram. And replaying that scene didn't make me afraid. It made me *angry*. Angrier than I'd been in almost a year. Now, though, I had power that I didn't have when Abram walked away from me. I was different. I was more.

I raised my hand to blast more energy at the dark creature, but before I could, his voice carried across the room.

"I need you," he said from Abram's lips. "I never should have left. It's not too late for us."

It was enough to give me pause. So badly, I wanted *this* vision to be true.

But the real Abram didn't want to be found. If he wanted me, I would have found him by now. The real Abram was gone, and all I could do was move on. Move on and save the people I still had left. It was one of the only things that I could do that would honor what he'd left me with. After all, when I'd first met him, Abram had been determined to keep the people of New Haven safe.

Even as I knew that, I lived every day with sharp regret for what I'd lost. Heartbreak would sneak up on me at the most unexpected times: while drinking a coffee and feeling the absence of having Abram to drink with; while in the shower, with nothing to distract me from the thoughts and heartache;

sometimes even while hunting down the evil in this world, missing the man I had first learned about my powers with.

Could I have done more to stop him from running away from me and what we had? Was there something more I could have said? I replayed that moment in my mind often; other times, it haunted me in dreams I'd rather not have.

I swallowed around the pinch in my throat, willing the tears not to fall. It was done. Abram was gone. I hadn't been able to stop him from leaving, and I hadn't found him during the year that I'd been searching. Now I was dealing with this creature, and in this moment, that was the only thing I could allow through the wall around my heart.

I walked over to the Shadow Elf, willing my power to spread through his body, regardless of the form he'd taken. "In case you haven't fully grasped what's happening here, let me make things clear," I said as he crashed to the floor. "I'm connected to Ramsey. He's my mage. That's what's up."

My connection to the power surged again, and the Shadow Elf grappled at his throat and looked at me with Abram's eyes. "Charisse…" he choked out. "Stop. It's me. I came back. I need your help. I'm trapped."

"Nice try, Shadow Douche. Here's the thing. When I hit you with that energy blast, it wasn't an offensive maneuver. I connected you to me, too. And, since we're all one big happy family now, that leaves something open to me."

In my peripheral vision, Ramsey was turning blue, and I realized that I didn't have time for all of this. My gut wrenched so hard I thought I would be sick. I needed to hurry. No way in hell was I going to lose another person I cared about to the evil of this world.

"I might not be able to undo what you're doing to Ramsey right now," I said, "but I *can* duplicate it. I can send the effects of that right to you if you don't stop it now." I stepped closer again, leveling a stare down at the elf, and trying not to see the face of my truest love looking back up at me, filled with pain and despair. "So, let me ask you, you ridiculous, disgusting creature: how do *you* like the idea of suffocating?"

The spell worked quickly, leaving my body and forcing its way around the Shadow Elf in a way that left even me impressed.

The Shadow Elf couldn't talk, of course. Perhaps in his normal state, he wouldn't need oxygen. But my spell bound him to the same earthly rules of whatever form he took. If Abram would need oxygen to live—and he would—then so did the Shadow Elf.

I hated to see Abram's face in pain. There was a part of me, a big part, that wanted nothing more than to run to that man, scoop him up, and make all his pain go away no matter what it cost me.

But this *wasn't* Abram. Abram was off in the great wide somewhere, looking for a new life. Hopefully somewhere safe. Hopefully not going through what his doppleganger was going through now.

The Shadow Elf slapped at the floor, shaking his head frantically.

"If you're not the bad guy, then you'll have to prove it," I said, my eyes moving quickly to Ramsey.

The Shadow Elf snapped his fingers while he stared at me with rage in his eyes, and Ramsey was free. He fell hard against the floor and grunted before greedily gulping up a few precious breaths.

I turned to the elf, snapped my fingers, and freed him like he'd just done for my friend. The Shadow Elf swallowed hard and looked up at me with furious eyes, and I could tell that he was contemplating how to get the upper hand.

"Don't even think of it," I said, reading his intentions. If he thought he was going to exact revenge on me, he had another think coming. "I'll put you right back where you were. Believe it."

To make my point, I snapped my fingers again, and the

floor beneath the Shadow Elf dissolved. He sank into it, and then it solidified again, trapping him in place.

"What the hell are you doing?" he hissed at me, looking around as he tried in vain to morph and free himself from the trap I'd put him in. "I did what you asked!"

"You're also the reason I had to ask it," I shot back. "And don't bother trying to shift. I turned that off by locking you into the form you're currently using. So, unless you want to spend the rest of eternity, or however long it is you things live, looking like the love of my life, then I suggest you continue doing as I ask."

"Huntsman's not the way you remember him, Charisse," the Shadow Elf said, shaking his head. "Things have happened that you don't know, and couldn't possibly understand. If you don't stop this ridiculousness, the entire world is going to face destruction." He swallowed hard. "If Satina were here, she'd tell you what needs to happen in a way that you would believe. I just don't have her skills."

"Stay out of my head!" I commanded the thing, figuring that was the way he knew about Satina, my dead Conduit frenemy. "If she were here, she'd know better than to think I could ever kill someone who means as much to me as Huntsman."

"Then she'd be wrong," a voice said from the darkness.

Looking up in the direction of the noise—a voice I would have recognized even if I was blind—I saw a window which had been closed just minutes ago was now open.

Someone had snuck in, and I hadn't even noticed.

A glowing purple arrow that was obviously laced in magic came flying from the darkness. It whizzed past me, and before I could make sense of what was going on, it struck the Shadow Elf in the chest and buried almost to the hilt.

The thing screamed. It sizzled as the magic pouring from the arrow seeped into the Shadow Elf's body in bright purple stripes. The thing exploded into a mess of black smoke and agony. The force of the explosion knocked me backwards, sending me onto my back and looking up at the ceiling.

Blinking hard, I looked up as a figure walked over to me from the shadows. My body shook as I took in what I was seeing.

Was this another trick? Had the Shadow Elf cast an extension of it's magic to conjure a visage? An illusion...a distraction...to come after me while my guard was down?

But as the figure stepped closer, there was something so undeniably true about what I was seeing that all my doubts melted away. When you're in the room with someone you love, you know if it's really them.

With an arrow gun in his hand and a scar across his face, I knew without a shadow of a doubt that the man I was looking at was Abram.

My Abram.

"One down," Abram said, pointing his arrow gun at the unconscious body of the Huntsman. "One to go."

CHAPTER 5

ONCE AGAIN, I couldn't believe what I was looking at. For the second time today, I was looking at the visage of the man I loved. This time was different, though. I wasn't sure exactly *how* I knew, but this was him. This was Abram.

While the Shadow Elf, who I had just watched disintegrate after being hit by a magic arrow, may have looked like Abram, this man did so much more than that.

The way he moved, the way he spoke, even the woodsy musk of him was the same as the man I loved. More than that, I *felt* something when I looked at him. Everything I hadn't felt in a year swelled up inside of me. Lifted me up and broke me down at the same time. A magnetic pull. A thousand emotions, most of which could not be formed into words because he'd destroyed me when he'd left.

The missing part of me was here, staring at me with dark eyes, and it was impossible to miss.

When the Shadow Elf turned into Abram, he screwed with a piece of my mind. This man was pinging at the deepest places in my heart, places that had been walled off since the night I watched Abram jump from that roof and out of my life. This couldn't be an illusion.

Was it possible? Could this man—the man who was poised to murder Huntsman right before my eyes—actually be Abram?

My mind was saying no, but my heart was saying something else entirely.

But even so, even as I was sure it really was Abram, there was something different about him. This wasn't the man or beast I remembered. For one, where did the magical crossbow come from?

"What are you doing?" I asked before I could stop myself, then swallowed hard and looked up at him.

Abram looked down at me. His eyes were the same as they had always been: the same shape, the same color, even the same intensity. But they held nothing more than that. The warmth I remembered seeing in those eyes when he looked at me was gone. There wasn't even a flicker of recognition as he stared at me.

"Just being a man, sweet thing," he said, shrugging. "More or less, anyway. I have no business with you. If you want to get your pathetic friend over there and hit pavement, I won't stop you," he said, motioning to Ramsey, who was still holding his throat and looking at Abram with wide eyes. "If you get in my way, though, I can't promise you'll make it out of here in one piece."

My heart shot right up into my throat, and once there, shattered into a million pieces. He didn't even acknowledge our history.

That very act was all the proof I needed that the man I was looking at right now was no cheap knockoff. No one who had ever lived could hurt me like this. No one could take my guarded heart, and with one sentence, reduce it to ash or shards in my chest. No one but him.

This was Abram. I knew it like I knew my own name.

But, if that was the case, what was going on here? Why was this happening? What the hell was he talking about?

"Abram?" I asked, the word shaky and my body trembling with some strange mixture of fear and anticipation.

Since the moment he left, all I had wanted was for him to return. All I wanted in the whole of the earth was to breathe the same air as him. Now that I was, I was more torn than ever.

"Is that his name?" Abram asked, motioning to Huntsman and smirking. "That's a bit more Old Testament than I was expecting. He looks like one of those new-age hipster dudes, with the long hair and pouty features." He shrugged. "I would have guessed Hunter or Lance; something fru-fru like that. Whatever. Abram can die just as easily as the rest of them."

"Charisse!" Ramsey yelled, scrambling to his feet. "He's not himself! You have to stop him! You have to—"

Abram's bow gun twitched, moving so that the business end of the arrow was pointed at Ramsey.

"I got one arrow left, bud," Abram growled. "I was gonna use it on the magic man over there, but seeing how he's taking a siesta right now, I can probably finish him off with my bare hands." The gun cocked. "I was going to let you go, but you don't seem like you're going to let me do my job in peace. So, you're going to have to get dead, my man."

These words—the phrases leaving Abram's mouth—didn't belong to him. He wasn't this man. He wasn't as contemporary and loose as all of this. His unique accent was gone, too. It was like I was talking to someone I'd grown up with in New Haven.

Abram was a timeless man. He was a three-piece-suit type of guy. He wouldn't be caught dead dressed as he was now. I should have known something was off when I saw him in a simple T-shirt and torn jeans. What was more, he wouldn't use these words to address anyone.

He knew me. He knew Ramsey and Huntsman. Whatever was happening here, it was screwing with who he was. I thought back to the spell, the sacrifice that he'd made, and I knew that had to be it.

I also knew that it was *not* okay with me.

"Charisse," Ramsey said uneasily. "Not to mess up whatever undoubtedly poignant thing is running through that head of yours right about now, but I'd rather not end up dead because of it." He looked over at me with huge eyes and sweat on his brow. "You think you might be able to help me out here?"

I couldn't move. I couldn't respond. This wasn't some weird Shadow Elf out to murder Ramsey. This was Abram. This was the man whose side I thought I would always be on, no matter what.

Except, I *couldn't* be on his side right now. Not with Ramsey's life on the line. Not with Abram making no sense at all. Not with the curse I knew that was running through his veins.

"I'm sorry," I said quietly, closing my eyes and casting the spell that would make us enemies.

As I did, the magic I commanded stripped him of his gun, throwing it across across the room. One more movement of my hand, and I knocked Abram back, too.

He flew through the air and slammed hard against the wall, cracking the plaster and shaking the entire building. I winced as I stood, every wound I was inflicting on his body mirroring itself in my soul. It was nearly enough to bring me to my knees.

I hadn't intended all that, but my emotions were in overdrive and affecting my ability to control my powers properly.

Scrambling to my feet, I finally took Abram in on equal footing. He recovered from his blow as quickly as I figured he might. He was, after all, a beast. His agility, his strength, his endurance—it was all far beyond that of a normal person's.

He had always been a physical specimen, and since he'd

REBECCA HAMILTON & CONNER KRESSLEY

left me, his powers were getting even stronger. There was no telling what he was capable of now. Unfortunately, judging by the look on his face, I would bet I was about to find out the hard way.

"You're a troublesome little thing, aren't you?" he asked, pulling a dagger from a belt across his waist I hadn't seen before. It, too, glowed with energy—this time green. "And to think, I was just going to let you and that man over there walk out of here. I'd have been a damn fool, wouldn't I? A Conduit like you is going to be worth a pretty penny on the black market." He blew a kiss at me. "Especially with a face like that." His eyes leered over my entire body. "And curves like those."

My entire being seemed to wretch. This wasn't right, and I needed to make sure he knew that.

"You know me, Abram," I said, powering up with my hands in front of me, just in case.

I wanted to bring some sense to the man, but if I couldn't, I'd be damned if I let Abram kill one of these men on my watch. I was going to get him back. I was sure of it. And once I did, he'd never forgive himself if either of their blood was on his hands.

I couldn't let that happen to him.

He took his time, looking between Ramsey and me, before he realized what I was saying.

"Is that me?" he asked, chuckling hard. "Is that who you think I am? Sweetheart, I think you have me confused with some lame ass-hat."

"You *are* Abram," I answered, my heart beating quickly. "You're Abram, I'm Charisse, and we belong together. Somewhere, deep inside, you must know that. Feel that."

I was getting desperate now, but I had to try and reach him.

That's how it worked in the movies, right? Seeing his one

true love, talking to her, would snap him out of it. It had to. Just like a fairytale.

"Yeah," he said, stepping toward me just slightly. "I kinda got that we were close, judging by the fact the smoke monster used my body to get your goat. I doubt we were as close as all that, though. I mean, I can't be sure, seeing as how the old noggin' hasn't worked in quite some time, and you're definitely my type, but I'm guessing I was more 'hit it and quit it.' I know girls can be like that sometimes, though. Clingy. That's probably why I left."

"You don't remember who you are?" I asked, my hands lowering a little instinctively as my heart went out to him. "You don't remember *anything*?"

"Of course I know who I am," he said. "It's who I used to be that proves to be troublesome." He shook his head as though he were trying to focus. "Don't worry, though. I couldn't be less interested in whoever the pansy ass bitch I used to be was. Though, if you had visions of white picket fences and a backyard with dog houses all across it, you might have to readjust your expectations." He shrugged again. "Or don't. In thirty seconds, your men are going to be dead, and you're going to be on your way to a life as an indentured servant to whoever will pay me the most for your magical, curvy ass."

With that, Abram took a threatening step toward me, dagger still in his hand, ready to rip through me like warm butter to get to the people I was standing stalwart to protect.

In that moment, looking at him, something in me shifted. The months and months of being on my own kicked in. All the changes in my life and in who I was, everything I had become in the time that he'd been gone, all of it came rushing over me and decimated the old me.

"I don't want to do this," I said, balling my hands into fists and pooling my energy inside of them. "I don't want to hurt you, but I will if that's what it takes."

In that moment, I knew that was exactly what I'd have to do, too.

Abram grinned at me as he lunged. I took a deep breath and thrust my fists outward. A wave of energy shot out, rushing in Abram's direction. It passed through him harmlessly, though, leaving him to continue on his path toward me, dagger in hand. I glanced down at my hands and cursed silently.

"That was cute," he said, leaping into the air and lifting the dagger into the air. "My turn."

With wide eyes, I tucked and rolled, letting him land on the other side of me. Then, I prepared for the battle that was going to happen next.

Standing, I saw that was exactly what he wanted. He turned from me and started toward Ramsey. Of course, my mage wasn't without defenses of his own. Looking over at him, I saw a gun in his hand.

"I'm sorry, Charisse," Ramsey said, his voice tense and firm. "I don't have a choice."

My heart sputtered as Ramsey raised the gun in Abram's direction. He couldn't. As a mage, he couldn't hurt someone, even if he tried.

Yet, somehow, Ramsey fired.

Twice.

My heart dropped to my gut and tried to come back up again, sure Abram was going to fall dead at my feet.

Instead, he moved that glowing dagger around like some kind of ninja, blocking both bullets like he was freaking Wonder Woman with those metal bracelets. He did a somersault in the air. As he landed, he kicked Ramsey in the face, knocking him down.

Ramsey had missed. I supposed the gun wouldn't have been able to fire if it was actually going to deliver a harmful blow. But Abram wasn't bound by the same magical rules as Ramsey. Abram *could* kill, and his sights were set on Ramsey.

"Abram! Don't you touch him!" I yelled.

If my powers were going to move through him uselessly, I would direct it back at me. I would use my magic to make myself strong enough to deal with Abram on his own, more physical terms.

"Don't worry, beautiful," Abram said, turning from Ramsey and heading toward Huntsman. "Business before pleasure, and all of that."

Grunting, I ran toward the man, watching Huntsman from the corner of my eye and wondering just how on earth he could seriously still be unconscious. He was a warrior, too —almost as powerful as Abram. Whatever happened to him before I got here, he should have definitely been up, around, and healed enough to be able to defend himself by now.

I slammed into Abram, knocking him out of Huntsman's path. Feeling the sting that came with our contact, I looked at Huntsman. In addition to his axe, which I wasn't about to try and wield, there was a sword hanging from his belt. I grabbed it, lifting it into a defensive position.

"I don't want to hurt you, Abram," I said again, my jaw tense.

"I love how you keep saying that, like it's a real possibility," he said, chuckling at me. "It's so damn cute."

He tossed the glowing dagger from one hand to the other, catching it and winking at me. "Whatever we were before, Charisse, I'm sure it was awesome. Judging from the way you fill out those jeans, I'm guessing I had a lot of fun. Just wish I could remember it. It might give me something to smile about after you're gone."

"I said I wouldn't hurt you," I said, blinking back tears. "But I'm also going to stop you. I swear it."

"Oh, baby," he muttered. "It just doesn't work that way."

He ran toward me again, and this time, I rushed in his direction, too. Ready to collide with the man I loved, a bright light appeared from underfoot. A swirling abyss materialized beneath me.

I knew instantly what it was, and I knew immediately who it came from. Ramsey had used one of his mystical doodads to open up a portal, and he was using it to swallow us up.

"Ramsey, no!"

But it was too late. The light had already swallowed me up.

When it was gone, I was standing in my apartment. Ramsey was beside me, and Huntsman lay on the floor.

Abram was gone, though, and there was no chance I could get him back.

CHAPTER 6

Ramsey had just portalled me away from Abram. I had searched for him for so long and hadn't been able to find him. That we had been in the same place at the same time had been nothing more than luck, and now that opportunity was gone forever.

I whirled toward Ramsey. "What the hell were you thinking?" I roared, tears in my eyes and fire in my veins.

"I was thinking," he said calmly, "that we needed to get the hell out of there before that man killed all three of us. That's what," he said, throwing his hands out as though I was being ridiculous.

Okay, so I was. That didn't change anything, though. "That *man* was Abram!"

I turned around rapidly, trying to figure out if there was a way that I could undo what Ramsey had just done. Unfortunately, there was nothing I could think of that would let me reverse engineer the portal.

"I know who he was," Ramsey interrupted. "I was there. I saw him. I felt the energy coming from him."

I crossed my arms. "Then what the hell was that?"

"That wasn't *all* he was," Ramsey said. "There wasn't *just* Abram there with us. You have to know that."

"If you knew him, then you should have known he wouldn't have killed us," I said. "He would never do that. He would never kill me."

Even as I said it, some part of me worried I was wrong. I didn't know what had happened to Abram in the past year, but he didn't seem open to considering my version of his past life. He didn't seem to recognize me *at all*. Not only that, but he was pretty adamant about killing both Ramsey and Huntsman.

"You don't know what he would do," Ramsey said, his tone turning gentle as if he already knew he was delivering the sad truth I was trying to deny. "He obviously had no idea who you were, and honestly, he didn't seem to care."

He was enough of a gentleman that he didn't point out that Abram had treated me like I was a gnat.

"Something happened to him," I said, tears pinching in the back of my throat. "That doesn't change who he is."

"Unless it does," Ramsey said quietly.

"What does that mean?" I asked, arching my eyebrows at the mage. Why did he have to make so much sense? Why did he have to make me question everything that I knew was true about Abram? The worst part was that he did it with three little words. Words that made me want to grab him by the throat and shake him like a ragdoll to get him to explain himself to me.

Ramsey didn't say anything for a few seconds. I could see the wheels turning in his mind as he tried to figure out the best way to get his point across. He'd had an entire year of dealing with me and my obstinate ways.

"It means I pointed a gun at him, Charisse," he finally answered, as though that made all the sense in the world.

"I know," I said. "I saw you." I struggled to keep my anger and rising outrage in check. I was there, I was part of the exchange. "And you've got a lot of nerve. How would you like it if I pointed a gun at Briar?"

"If she was trying to murder you, I'd expect it," he answered simply. He didn't bring up the fact that I had actually been at odds with the love of his life not that long ago. "But you're missing the point." He shook his head. "I'm a mage, Charisse. You know the rules I live by. The rules that I'm bound to obey by blood and magic. I'm not capable of killing a person. I shouldn't have even been able to get as far as I did with that gun. Pointing it at him should have been physically impossible."

My heart skipped a beat as I took in what Ramsey was saying. He was right. He was absolutely right. I'd seen Ramsey completely unable to harm someone who meant to kill others, and it had hurt him when he tried. I'd seen him struggle with his limitations a lot over the past year, and he never got as close to hurting someone like he'd gotten with Abram. So, what did it mean that he was able to aim a gun at Abram with the intent to fire it?

"What are you saying, Ramsey?" I asked, narrowing my eyes at him and demanding an explanation. "That there's no good left in him? That he can't be saved?"

I held my breath, knowing what Ramsey was going to say next, but not wanting to hear it. Changing everything about who I was didn't take away the fact that I wanted the man I loved to be there. To be whole.

"I'm saying that whatever Abram has been through in the time since we've seen him has changed him, and not for the better," Ramsey replied, taking a step toward me. "When he left, his powers were evolving and changing because of the darkness inside him. I think that evolution has made him less human, less of who he's always been. It's certainly screwed with his essence enough to make it possible for me to hurt him if I wanted to." Ramsey's wire-framed glasses slid a fraction down his nose, but he didn't move to correct them. "Not that I could. I mean, he's a deadly thing. The way he outmaneuvered the bullets I shot at him was incredible, to say the least."

"He's human," I said, glaring at the mage and refusing to acknowledge the truth in his words. My jaw ached from clenching my teeth, and my heart thudded like a bass drop in a New York night club. "I mean, of course he's a human. What else would he be? That's a ridiculous thing to say."

"Is it ridiculous, Charisse? Or does it make more sense than you want to face? Especially when it comes to Abram."

Ramsey sighed as he flopped down onto my apartment couch. The sofa was secondhand and beat to hell. Something I never would have owned before meeting Abram. But it'd reminded me of one of the sofas from his club back in New Haven, even though worse for wear, and I couldn't pass it up.

"And you know what else he'd be, Charisse," Ramsey continued. "You've seen all sorts of monsters since this began. You know the depths to which he might have slid."

A sick feeling ran through me. It was so sharp, so intense, that I struggled to actually breathe through it. The idea that not only was Abram gone from me, but he was also gone from himself was enough to destroy me completely.

"It's not true," I said. If he had devolved into something that much less than human, then he truly was never coming back to me. I couldn't accept that. "I can get him back." I slapped my hands together. "I have to get him back. We got Charlie back, so Abram can be saved too."

"You don't know that," Ramsey said with a shake of his head. I could tell he was getting frustrated, just as angry as I was.

"And you don't know that I can't!" I shot back, pointing a finger at the mage which was enveloped in the sort of offensive magic that—even now—I would have never used against him. The fact that I was 'on' like that only served to prove how upset I really was. My magic was never this difficult.

Ramsey seemed unaffected as he took off his glasses, closed his eyes, and tipped his head against the back of the couch. He looked exhausted. That, or defeated.

For a moment, I felt bad that I was the cause of his exhaustion, but he'd been the one to send me into the abandoned building in the first place. He was the one that started this.

"You don't even know that you'll be able to find him for a second time," he declared. After cleaning his glasses on his shirt, he put his glasses back on and looked at me again. "Hell, you didn't even find him the first time. He found you."

"I'm a fucking phenomenon, Ramsey. There's never been anything like me in the whole of this damned magical world. So, how about you stop telling me what I can and can't do and focus on your job."

Again, I was ignoring the fact that he was only telling me the truth. I was just too upset to listen. Plus, I was insulting him the only way I knew how.

"My *job*?" he asked, his eyes widening and his face losing much of its color as he sat up and focused intently on me. "My job took a back seat when you started throwing yourself in front of every bullet that came shooting by."

I took several bold steps toward him and posted my hands on my hips. "What are you talking about?" I did nothing to hide the fact that I was insulted that he was calling me out on the dangerous things I'd been doing, for the entire city.

"You, Charisse," he said, indicating me with a wave of his hand. "You think this is the first time I've been prepared to rush across town to save your ass? Didn't you wonder how I got there so quickly? It's because I was already on the way when you cut out on me."

"You followed me?" I asked, then swallowed hard.

Where was all of the trust I'd earned in the past year?

Why did I feel like he was treating me as though I was the same innocent girl in New Haven?

"I always follow you," he admitted. "Ever since you lost Abram, you've been so damn eager to die that it takes all I can not to lock you in a padded room and throw away the key."

"You're insane," I snapped. "I don't want to die. Why the hell would you say that?"

"Because you act like you do, Charisse," he answered, sitting up and moving to the edge of his seat. He clasped his hands together by his knees and leaned back to make eye contact with me. "You act like your life isn't worth anything, like you don't care whether you live or die." His eyes welled up with tears, and his Adam's apple bobbed before he looked away. "Some of us do care, Charisse. Some of us care very much whether you live or die."

"I get it," I said bitterly. "I'm important for saving the world and all that crap."

"Fuck the world." This time, when his attention snapped back to me, his expression was full of anger. "That's secondary, and honestly it's a bigger conversation than I can have on my own. I care about you because you are my *friend*. End of story." He shook his head. "If you'd pull your head out of that sea of self-pity you've been forcibly drowning in for months now, you might see that a lot of people feel the same way as I do."

"I didn't mean to come across like I didn't care about you, about anyone," I said. I thought of the funk I'd fallen into as many things over the months. Never once had I thought of it as selfish. "And I don't want to die, regardless of how much it might look that way."

"Then why?" he asked. "Why are you acting the way you are, Charisse?"

"Because I have to make it worth something," I said. "Abram left to save me, to give me a good life."

"You think fighting monsters is a good life?" He tossed his

hands up and shot to his feet. He strolled over to the window, his back turned to me and his arms crossed.

"Good lives are for children and the Amish," I said to the back of his head. "I'm a grown-up. I owe it to the world, I owe it to myself, and I owe it to Abram to make his sacrifice worth something. I have to make my life worthwhile. Otherwise, all of this has happened for no reason at all."

"With all due respect, I'm not sure Abram would agree with that," Ramsey said, his voice softening. He still didn't turn to face me, though. "I'd wager that, if you asked him, he'd say you with a couple of fat grandchildren and a life full of good memories is all he'd want from this."

"Well, we can't ask him, can we?" I said, shaking my head and blinking back tears. "Like you said, he's gone." Just like the last time he vanished from my life, I was left crushed by Abram's absence.

Finally Ramsey turned back to face me.

"Maybe not," he said, causing my heart to jump. Hadn't I *just* said that? Now, he might have a plan.

"What?" I shook my head to make sure I was understanding him correctly. "What do you mean by that? Explain." I couldn't stop talking long enough for him to answer, because he wasn't answering fast enough. "Ramsey?"

When I'd said it, we both knew I was desperate not to lose the man I loved. Ramsey, well, he would only say it if there was a possibility.

"You told me to do my job," he said. "I might as well oblige. I'm sure there's been a case like Abram's at some point in the recorded history of magic. It'll probably take a lot of digging," he said, spreading his hands, "but I'm damn good with a shovel."

He strode over to me until he was standing at my side but facing the opposite direction. "We'll find something," he said, placing his hand on my shoulder. "And now that I know what kind of magical signature I'm looking for, I might even be able to find Abram himself."

I couldn't stop the tears from running down my face. I'd waited so long to hear those words. I'd pleaded countless times that there had to be a way to help him. Before now, Ramsey hadn't seen a way. He cared about me enough not to get my hopes up. If he said something could be done now, then he must mean it.

Emotions flooded me so hard and fast, I didn't know what to do with myself. All I knew was that I wanted to thank him. But when I opened my mouth to talk, another voice stopped me.

"Charisse?" Huntsman called as he stumbled out of the bedroom where we'd moved him while he was unconscious.

I stared at him while he rubbed his head as though he was struggling to understand what was happening.

"Where am I? How did I get here?" He blinked at me. "Oh," he said while looking around. "Where is my blasted genie?"

CHAPTER 7

I LOOKED AT HUNTSMAN, my mind spinning and my body more tense than it had a right being. Staring at him, I knew that nothing I had been through in the last few hours even penetrated the surface of what he'd been forced to endure.

The huge man, large with broad shoulders and biceps that must have been custom-made for either fighting or showing off, stumbled toward me, using the wall to hold himself up. He looked drunk, beaten and severely abused.

I had seen Huntsman in a fight or two during the time I'd known him, but I had never seen anything mess with him like this. What was more, he was spouting nonsense about a genie.

I needed to steady him. After that, I'd figure out just how he'd gotten to that abandoned building and why the Shadow Elf was so afraid of him.

"You need to sit down, Huntsman," I said, taking his arm gently and leading him toward the couch. "Can you put on some coffee, Ramsey?" I asked, looking over at the mage. "Something tells me this is going to be a longer night than I thought."

Once I had Huntsman on the couch and a cup of strong black coffee in his hands, I figured it was time to get down to what was really going on. As it turned out, Huntsman had a similar idea.

Pulling the cup from his lips, he cut me off with his question. "How did I get here?"

While Huntsman waited for an answer, he turned and stared at me with eyes that told me that he'd been through hell and back.

"We brought you here," I said quickly. "Ramsey and I were tracking a pretty intense magical signature. We traced it to a building on the bad side of town and, when I got there, you were unconscious lying in a corner."

I left out the part about the Shadow Elf and everything else that had happened.

"What?" he asked, sitting up a bit straighter. "That's impossible."

"Judging by the last couple of years, I'm going to go ahead and say that we stop using that word," I muttered. "I find it doesn't really mean much when we're always pitted against the things we have been." Shaking my head, I continued, "You were being attacked by a Shadow Elf, and then...then by someone else. I just need to know how you got there, and what's going on. The magical signature that's coming off of you doesn't match anything we know about you, Huntsman. The Shadow Elf was afraid. He was freaking terrified that you might wake up and be—"

"Starving," Huntsman said, standing up quickly, his eyes roaming my living room frantically.

"What? No," I said, standing myself. "He was afraid—"

"I'm starving, Charisse," he said. "I can't explain it, but I'm hungrier than I've ever been in my life. I feel like I'm going to drop dead if I don't get something to eat right now."

He ran into my kitchen in what had to be one of the strangest displays I'd ever seen in my life. I just watched him go, and then decided I should probably follow him and give him something to eat before he destroyed my kitchen.

"Fine," I said as he pulled a half rack of ribs from my freezer and slammed it down on the bar.

He ripped the packaging open, pulled off a meaty rib, and raised it toward his mouth.

"Huntsman!" I said, springing across the room to grab the rib. I tried to pull it out of his grasp, but he was too strong. "It's still raw!"

"I don't care! I'm starving!" he said, jerking the slab of meat back so quickly that he knocked me backward. He dug his teeth into the meat and ripped a piece of it off the bone like some caveman right out of the Stone Age.

"Stop!" I said. Twisting my wrist, I magically pulled the bone from his hand and forced it to the counter. With another twist, the ribs instantly cooked on the counter. In a second, they were ready. "There. At least you won't catch anything now."

Huntsman looked at me, blinking hard as if he was coming back to himself. "I-I'm sorry, Charisse. I have no idea what came over me."

"Neither do I," I admitted, leaning against the counter. "Tell me what happened. How did you get to that building?" I motioned toward the meat. "And go ahead. It seems like you need it."

Huntsman practically groaned as he bit into the cooked ribs. He moaned so loudly and with so much satisfaction that I was sure my neighbors would be talking about it tomorrow.

"Huntsman, focus, please," I said, pushing a blush down from my cheeks.

"I don't know," he said, wiping grease from his face. "The last thing I remember, I was in Alaska, fighting off a pack of wolves and trying to keep them from tearing my face off. Lydia was with me, and I told her I needed help. After that, everything was a blur."

"Lydia?" I asked, chewing at my lip. "Who's Lydia?"

Ramsey walked into the kitchen and eyed the mountain of

bones Huntsman was quickly compiling with each rib he polished off. "I'm going to guess she's the genie you mentioned when you woke up," Ramsey said.

"Genie?" I asked, practically scoffing at the idea. "Genies aren't real, are they?" I looked from one of them to the other hoping they'd tell me I wasn't crazy. "I mean, there's no way that's real. I'd have heard about them by now."

"They're real," Ramsey said with a pitying look in his eyes. "They're rare, but they're real, nonetheless." His gaze turned to Huntsman, and the look on his face was much more dire than I might have expected. "They're also horribly dangerous. At least, some of them are. Where did you find your genie, Huntsman?"

"On the ocean floor," he said without missing a beat, as though that was a normal thing to say. "I was looking for an artifact to depower a particularly troublesome coven of witches, and an oracle told me I'd find what I needed there. What I came up with was a brass lamp that housed a brown-haired woman who was as beautiful as she was powerful."

"I doubt that very seriously," Ramsey said. "Genies are some of the most powerful creatures in the universe. Legend has it that they're made from the same energy that formed life on this planet." He shook his head. "Which is to say, that woman would have to be pretty damn beautiful to match that kind of powerset."

"In any event," I said, trying to steer the conversation away from the way the woman looked, because I really didn't want to slap them right now. "What happened next?"

"She introduced herself and told me I was her new master," he said. "I told her I wasn't looking for that kind of relationship, but she wouldn't exactly take no for an answer. She informed me that the binding between genie and master could only be broken after the master uses up three wishes." He ran a hand through his long hair. "I rattled off a few wishes quickly, but she told me that wasn't how it worked. The wishes had to be true wishes. They had to be 'worthy,' whatever that means."

"It means that genies aren't stage magicians," Ramsey said. "They don't perform for your amusement. Power as earth-shattering as the sort that runs through a true genie is to be treasured and is only released when the master is in dire need or asking for something that is truly from the heart. That's what makes it worthy, and I'm guessing you figured that out already and used up all three worthy wishes."

"How did you know that?" Huntsman asked, narrowing his eyes at the man.

"Because of what's happening to you," he said. "Genies are notorious tricksters. They're known for telling half truths and for twisting things to benefit themselves. What your genie didn't tell you, Huntsman, was that the reason the bond between the genie and the master is broken after the third wish, is because the master takes the genie's place."

"What?" I swallowed hard. "So, you're saying that the reason Huntsman was giving off that insane magical signature—"

"Is the same reason he's experiencing that ravenous hunger," Ramsey said. "His body is changing. He's turning into a genie."

EVERYTHING around me was spiralling out of control. First Abram was stolen away and transformed into something else. Now, Huntsman was turning into a genie. While Huntsman didn't mean nearly as much to me as Abram did, I couldn't escape one undeniable connection between the men: *me.*

Huntsman held out a tall glass of water as he brushed a stray strand of hair from my face.

"Are you all right?" he asked, as I took the glass from his hands.

I took three gulps of water before realizing how slimy the glass felt and set the water aside, staring at the grease of the ribs that had transferred from Huntsman's hands onto my glass.

Huntsman pinned me with his gaze, as if I were the one who had just received the life-shattering news and not him. But I wasn't the one whose body was turning on me. I wasn't the one who was being changed into something against my will, into something I didn't understand.

"I'm fine," I said, forcing a smile up at him. I grabbed a paper towel and wiped down the glass, as if having control over the grease would give me some kind of peace. God knows I didn't have control over anything else in my life. "I should be the one asking you that question, you know. You're the one who's going through something horrible."

"I can deal with horrible, Charisse," Huntsman said. "I'm familiar with horrible. She's an old friend of mine. What I would rather not have to acquaint myself with is the idea that you're going to be hurt by this."

"How could I not?" I asked, lying back on the couch and tossing my arm across my eyes. "You're turning into a genie."

"A djinn," Ramsey cut in, rummaging through books on the kitchen table with the eraser end of a pencil in his mouth. "A female genie is a djiniri and a male genie is called a djinn."

"I don't give a damn what you call it," I whined under my breath. "I don't want to lose anyone to it, regardless of what it's called."

"You don't know that you will lose me, Charisse," Huntsman said sternly. "Your mage assures me there is a way to undo this calamity, and even if there isn't, we have no idea what happens after one is transformed into a djinn. Perhaps it will be a pleasant experience."

I practically snorted out a laugh, though truthfully, there was nothing funny about it. Had he already forgotten the events that led him here?

"You'll be sucked into the lamp you found on the ocean floor, where you'll remain, suffering in the dark, until someone the lamp deems worthy finds you, releases you, and forces you to do their bidding, regardless of what it is," I said, reminding him of what he'd told me. "If the person you'll have to call master isn't aware of the way this works, he or she will make three true wishes, and you'll be freed so they can take your place. If they are, though, they'll seal you back in the lamp after two wishes, where you'll wait—again, suffering in the dark—until someone else worthy finds you and the process repeats itself. So, all in all, no, I doubt very much it's going to be a pleasant experience."

Huntsman looked over at Ramsey, blinking hard at the man. "You couldn't have just lied to save the woman's feelings?"

"I don't want to be lied to," I said, removing my arm from my eyes and sitting up. My hands curled around the edge of the couch cushion. "I want to be in this thing, damn it. I know I freaked out a little when I heard everything, but I'm here now, and I'm your best chance at getting around this." I rose to my feet, and Huntsman did the same. "I'm powerful. Much more powerful than I was the last time you saw me."

"I'm aware," Huntsman said. "Tales of your escapades and The Brothers' dogged attempts at your life reached me even in the far-off kingdom of Alaska."

"So, I hate to break it to you. Alaska's not so much a kingdom as a state, although I guess that's not really the point," I said. "What I'm getting at is: if there's a spell that can fix this, I'm your girl."

"In a different life, perhaps you would have been," Huntsman said, with a winsome smile across his nearly perfect face. Then, he went and ruined it by winking at me.

I smiled as I gazed at the scar that now ran across his cheek.

"How did you get that?" I asked, brushing my fingers across the blemish.

"It doesn't matter," he said, grabbing my hand and holding it in place on his cheek. "I will wear it proudly, as a warrior does." He sighed, releasing me and taking a step back. "I always thought I would receive the honor of a noble death, that I would die in battle, that it would be worth it, that children would tell my stories through generations." He shook his head. "I never imagined my tale would end as a magical slave to whoever a bottle deems as worthy to use me."

"It's a lamp, not a bottle," Ramsey interjected, still looking at the books. "And a spell's not going to do it, I'm afraid. At least, not *just* a spell."

He turned the book in his hand around, laying it on the table turned toward us, and we crossed the room together to look at the pages as Ramsey continued.

"These are stories of people going through what you're going through now, Huntsman. The transformation always happens the same way." He started pointing with a pencil to illustrations on the page as he spoke. "Once the bond is broken and the master becomes the djinn, he's cast into a deep sleep. When he awakes from that sleep, he has three days before the bottle takes him in forever. Those three days are the only window we have. I've found exactly one mention of someone being able to undo the transformation once it's started, and he did it within the three-day window, but only barely."

"How?" I asked, a flicker of hope lighting up in me as I turned to stare at him. "How did he do it?"

"He found the genie whose place he was taking and forced her back inside the bottle. Because she had been in it before, the bottle recognized her and imprinted on her when the window closed." Ramsey took off his glasses, cleaned them on the hem of his shirt, and stuck them back on. After clearing his throat, he continued. "But it won't be easy. Huntsman might have the power signature of a djinn, but the actual powerset doesn't transfer until the three-day window closes. Which means—"

"The genie still has her magic," I finished.

"Right," Ramsey said. "So all we have to do is find one of the most powerful creatures in the world and somehow force her to do something she'd probably kill us all for even suggesting."

"Simple enough," I quipped, my stomach twisting into knots. "What are we going to do?"

"The genie is so powerful that she borders on not human," Ramsey said. "We have to find someone else who shares that similarity, someone whose powers might actually match that of the genie's, someone so brazen and confident in his abilities that he'd actually rush into a room where he thought a genie was present and try to kill her without a second thought."

"Oh my God." My heart raced. "You're talking about—"

"That's right," Ramsey said. "We have to bring in the big guns. It's time we find Abram, and this time on purpose."

Finding Abram was what I had wanted for so long. But not for the purpose of risking his life and losing him all over again.

Besides, how on earth were we going to convince him to help us after what had just happened between us?

CHAPTER 8

IT HAD BEEN AN HOUR, and though we didn't have much time to waste, I needed to be alone. That's why I cut out of our apartment to go for a run. And that's why I didn't stop running, even after my lungs began to burn as much as my legs.

After everything that had happened, the idea of pulling Abram into all of this was just too much. No, it was more than that. If I was being completely honest with myself, there was another reason I was having such a bad reaction to all of this, and it made me feel really damn guilty.

But before I could deal with the wild emotions coursing through me, Ramsey walked up behind me in an alley that happened to be on the complete other side of town than where our home was.

"What are you doing?" he asked.

His voice easily carried over the clattering and clanging of the city and the hum of traffic just outside the alley. Ramsey was generally a soft-spoken man, so whenever he raised his voice, even if was only to be heard more easily, I knew he was serious and wanted my attention.

"Trying to outrun all of this, I guess," I said, shooting

sparks of energy into an overturned dumpster—the same thing I had been doing for the last thirty minutes. "I messed up, Ramsey. All of it just got messed up."

"What do you mean?" He strolled closer, but paused before coming to my side. "I get this is a lot to take in. And I understand that Huntsman is in danger. But I honestly imagined the idea of finding Abram again would be the one bright spot in all of this. Isn't that what you've wanted all this time?"

I turned to the mage, a mix of anger, astonishment, and disappointment in the fact that, after everything, he didn't know me better than that.

"Is that what you thought?" I asked, scrunching my nose. Not because the alley smelled like rotten dumpster food—which it did—but because I was offended to the point of disgust by his question. "Seriously?"

Ramsey held his hands out complacently. "He's the love of your life, Char."

"You're damn right he is." I blinked back a near torrent of tears. "That's why I was hoping he was out of all of this."

I cupped my face with my hands and breathed heavy into them, trying to stop myself from shaking.

"I was hoping he had a different life," I continued. "I used to lay awake at night, when the pain was so great that I was afraid it was going to rip me in half. When that happened, the only thing that made me feel like I was going to survive was the idea that he was better off than being stuck next to me and all the crazy that comes with my life. I thought that, without me, he might actually be able to have a good life. I thought he might be happy and free. I thought, if that happened, all of this garbage might actually be worth it and that I could fade away."

I dropped my hands along with the pretense that I'd ever be able to stop the tears from streaming down my face. While the tears fell uncontrollable, I did my best to ignore them and continued. "It wasn't worth it, though. It was all for nothing. All this fight, all this sacrifice, and he's still trapped here in the darkness. He's no better off than he was before."

"Oh, Charisse," Ramsey said, stepping over a puddle that might not actually be rainwater to come closer and wrap me in a comforting hug.

His heartbeat thudded against my chest, and for the first time in a long time, I didn't feel quite as alone. Even surrounded by people like we constantly were in a city like this one, I always felt like I was by myself. In a matter of seconds, Ramsey changed that.

"Of course he's already in the darkness if he's without you," Ramsey said quietly. "Don't you get it, sweetie? You were always his light." He pulled away from me, looking me deep in the eyes. "Now, come on. I know this is hard, and I know you feel like all of your work has boiled down to nothing, but that couldn't be further from the truth. The truth is, you're the only thing keeping this whole damn world from falling into decay. Now, we just have to figure out how to handle what's next."

"That's nice of you to say." I sniffled and looked up at him as I wiped my eyes with my wrists.

"It's the truth, and there's nothing nice about it," Ramsey said. "When I met you, do you know I thought you were little more than a spoiled former model?"

"That's probably because your wife hated me," I said, chuckling and thinking about Briar, my old nemesis and Ramsey's beloved. "And because that's pretty close to accurate."

"Briar had her own set of priorities back then," the man said. "As she does now, and it breaks my heart that I can't be with her."

"I'm so sorry about that." A flash of guilt ran through me as I remembered the conversation I'd had with Ramsey, the one where he decided it was too dangerous to be with his wife at a time like this, when the Brothers were after me and when he'd deemed it his responsibility to train me for the fight that was to come.

"Don't you dare be sorry," he answered. "I know that, in a perfect world, you'd much rather be with the person you love, raising babies and eating at fancy restaurants. Circumstances have dictated that things like that are impossible for the both of us right now, and that isn't your fault. The fate of the world hangs heavy on the shoulders of those who are tasked with it. If Satina were here, she'd tell you just how proud of you she was." Ramsey waited a bit. "So would your mother."

I took a deep and steadying breath, because I knew what would come next. My mind cleared. Like Satina before him, Ramsey had a way of cutting down to the quick of things when it came to me. With a single phrase, or even a flick of his eyebrow, he could convey exactly what I needed to hear. It was like a magic power he had, and it seemed to come in handy way more than the bag of tricks that were at my own disposal.

"We have work to do," I said determinedly. "And not nearly enough time to do it."

"That's true," Ramsey said. "But, before we do that, there are things to consider. Things that are extremely important and often overlooked."

I took a step back from the mage. "What sort of things?"

"The sorts of things that would affect whether you actually want to move forward with this," he said and sighed loudly. "The djinn is among the rarest of races in the supernatural world. Their powers are both immense and hard to control. Because of that, most of them were either hunted down and destroyed or banished off-world long ago. In fact, they are so rare that, for centuries, many of the smartest people in the world considered them extinct."

"Okay," I said, narrowing my eyes. Where was he going with this? It didn't change the facts. "I guess the smartest people in the world were wrong. Lord knows it wouldn't have been the first time. I mean, I didn't think they were real, either."

"That's not what I'm saying, Charisse." He sighed again, this time through his nose. "Djinns are rare, and the fact that Huntsman, someone who is as close to you as almost anyone in the world, came across one and found himself entangled with it, seems like quite the large coincidence to me."

My heart skipped a beat as I looked him up and down, finally understanding just what he was getting at. "Are you saying that this might be a setup? Are you insinuating that Huntsman might have been used as a pawn by someone?"

It went without saying that if he was used as a pawn, it was to get closer to me.

"Not just someone," Ramsey said sternly, looking at me unblinkingly. "I'm saying this could have come from The Brothers themselves."

While everything around me and the craziness of the past few hours finally clicked into place, my mind started to race. "Why would you think that?" I paced the alleyway, my shoes scuffing over the pavement. Long gone were my designer heels; I'd finally traded them in for some Chucks. "There's no proof of that."

"They're rare, Charisse," he said. "Rarer than you know."

"Well I didn't think they existed before today, so I don't know about that." I laughed sardonically. "But even if so, who cares?" I asked, throwing my hands into the air. "A lot of things are rare. Do you think four-leaf clovers come from The Brothers, too?"

"Don't be ridiculous." Ramsey scoffed. "Everyone knows four-leaf clovers are inventions of the Druids."

"Ramsey!" I balked. Why did he have to constantly ruin things that were important or magical to me? Sheesh.

"I'm just saying that we need to be careful," he continued. "We need to consider every possibility and the outcome of those possibilities." He stepped toward me again, close enough to lean against the dumpster before quickly thinking the better of it and straightening himself to dust off his jacket. "If this is a trap laid out by The Brothers—"

"Then they picked the perfect bait," I said, my voice hard and unwavering. "Because I'm not going to let Huntsman die."

"He wouldn't die," Ramsey corrected me.

"No. It would be worse than that," I amended. "He'd live forever in some horrible torment. It would be hell, Ramsey, and I'm not about to let my friend go to hell." I shook my head. "Even if it means my life."

"What if it means *everyone's* lives?" He let the question hang in the air between us, seeping into my bones and churning in my gut. "What you're not taking into consideration is that you're bigger than just yourself. You are, in no small way, the one hope of peace in our world. You're the connection between the Suppliants and the Conduits. You're the ticket to being out from under the thumb of the Brothers. You're as damn close to a queen as I've ever seen."

"I'm not a queen," I said immediately.

I couldn't have anyone counting on me like that. Once upon a time, I'd thought that being royalty would be awesome...but now, not so much after everything I'd seen.

"Tell that to the people counting on you," Ramsey said. "Tell it to the future generations, who dream of growing up in a world of peace and prosperity. Tell it to the people who look to you, who hear your story and have hope." He looked down at the ground. "And, while you're at it, tell them that the life of your friend is more important than they are."

I saw it—the condemnation in his eyes. The way he thought that I would actually choose one person's life over the rest of the world.

"That's not what this is about," I whispered, dejected. As much as I wanted to say that it wasn't, we both knew that everyone else would see it that way.

"I'm afraid that may not be how they see it." Ramsey strolled a few paces away from the dumpster, hands tucked in his pockets. He didn't look at me as he spoke. "What happened to Huntsman was unfortunate, but it's not a world-ending problem. In fact, if I had to pick someone to wield the powers of the djinn, I'd want it to be someone with that man's temperament."

"Except it wouldn't be his temperament. It would be whatever madman found his bottle." I pointed a finger at Ramsey. "Besides, it's wrong. Huntsman is my friend, and I won't let an innocent man suffer. What kind of person would I be if I let that happen?"

"I'm not sure," Ramsey said, stealing a quick glance over his shoulder at me before looking toward the ground again. "But something tells me I'll never have to find out."

"You're damn right," I said, nodding firmly and crossing my arms. "I know I have responsibilities to the world, but I also have responsibilities to myself. I have to be able to look at myself in the mirror. I have to be able to sleep at night. I have to know I'm not doing this for nothing." I ran a hand through my hair. "I just have to."

"I understand that, and I respect it," Ramsey said. He stood with his back to me for a long moment before turning to face me again. "But, keep in mind, this won't be easy. Even if this isn't a trap, and I'm not convinced that it isn't, having Abram back in his current state will be difficult for you. He was going to kill you when we last met. He would have succeeded if I hadn't gotten us portaled out of there."

"I can't think about that right now," I said, closing my eyes and trying to ignore the fact that he was right. "Let's just find him. Then we'll deal with the fact that he wants me dead, or at least wants to hurt me." I sighed, and then smiled as best as I could. "One impossible task at a time, right?"

Opening my eyes, I found Ramsey smirking at me. "Seems all in a day's work for the great Charisse Bellamy."

"Don't oversell me," I muttered.

"Oh, Charisse," he said, and there was something like pride in his eyes as he took me in. "I don't think that's possible."

"I wish I had your confidence," I grumbled again, shaking my head and thinking about all the things I had been through in the last year.

I had gotten through so much that no one should have been able to survive. But the thing was, I got through them mostly because of Abram—not by any great skill of my own. Now he was gone, and the thing taking his place bore very little resemblance to the man I loved. There was no way that I could do all this on my own.

The idea of soldiering on the way I always had was more than a little troublesome. What if I *couldn't* do this? What if I found that, on my own, I was no match for the horrors that lay in my path? What if the terrible things that were out there haunted me every step of the future?

"I think," Ramsey said, smiling a little and breaking through the darkness that had overtaken me, "when you need it, it will come."

And, just like that, I really believed that I wasn't alone.

I might not have had Abram, at least not Original Recipe Abram, but I had my friends. What was more, I was still Charisse Bellamy, damn it, and that meant something.

The only problem was, none of that changed the dangers that lay ahead, and I couldn't shake the unease churning in my stomach.

Would I really risk the entire world to save one person?

CHAPTER 9

I SHUFFLED UNEASILY to the small kitchen table as I tried to zip up a dress I hadn't worn in over a year. I couldn't get it the last bit, but I turned around and lifted my hair while Ramsey silently did it the rest of the way up.

I spun back to face him, more confused than ever. "I'm not sure I understand what's happening here," I said, smoothing some of the wrinkles in my dress above my thighs. "You said we were going to find Abram. What does that have to do with a candlelit dinner?"

In front of me was a plate of spaghetti that looked more than a little al dente, burned garlic bread, and mashed together meatballs that would have made my Italian grandmother roll over in her grave while asking me why I would hurt her like this with such subpar food.

What was more, Ramsey insisted on me wearing this dress, a white number that hugged my ample curves in all the right ways and plunged at both the neckline and in the back.

It was certainly a sexier dress than I would have worn to cast a spell, maybe even the seierst dress that I had worn since before Abram had left. Although, as I stood there in the kitchen, I couldn't help but feel like I was back in my element.

After all, I'd spent the majority of my adult life walking down runways wearing less clothing than this.

At least I knew that I looked good, regardless of whatever craziness Ramsey would have me doing.

"This *is* the spell," Ramsey said, taking a black candle—a relic that Satina had taught me held much in the way of dark energy—and lighting it before setting it between us.

"This?" I asked, looking down at myself and grimacing. The truth was, I did look damn good in my dress, and it'd been a long time since I'd gotten this dolled up. I'd even gotten my nails done and painted a deep coral for the first time since I'd began training with Ramsey. "Me getting all dressed up and sitting down to a frankly pretty crappy dinner is part of the spell? No offense," I said, "but I could have made better spaghetti in my sleep."

"Well, then you should have," Ramsey snarked.

I sat down across from him. To any outsider, it would look like two friends sharing a meal. Him eating the spaghetti. Me pushing the pasta around on the cheap white plate with my fork. Just two friends having dinner...not some dark magic spell.

"Doesn't this seem familiar to you?" he asked, chuckling softly. He wiped his mouth with a napkin. "I wouldn't take offense to the dinner, because you were the one who made it. At least, a year or so ago, you did."

I balked. "I did what?"

Then, looking at the scene with fresh eyes, it came back to me. This dinner, this dress, this table setting—it was all a replica of a date I had with Abram last year. I'd made such a mess of the dinner because I didn't know how to cook then. Well, that and the fact I was so giddy about being able to spend time with Abram.

As I took all of this in, I unexpectedly found myself blinking back tears. All of the memories hit me like a ton of bricks, and I didn't know what to do.

I took my first bite of the spaghetti Ramsey had cooked, and somehow it tasted better than I remembered, even though it looked just as bad as it had when I ruined it. Maybe that was the nostalgia kicking in, because I knew for a fact that it was still terrible.

"I was going through your photo album when you were gone," Ramsey said by way of explanation.

Huntsman walked in with two dessert plates of tiramisu in his hands, crossing the yellow kitchen floor tiles. "Something of which I completely disagreed with," he said. "Going through your things, I mean. Not the food. I'm still starving."

"The dessert was garbage, too," I said almost wistfully.

"The scent certainly speaks to that." Huntsman sniffed and set the plates on the counter in a similar position to where they'd been the night this actual date took place. It'd been from the freezer aisle, so I'd had it set aside to thaw while we ate at the kitchen table, all the while hoping Abram wouldn't object too loudly.

"It's okay," I said, blinking hard and taking a deep breath. "The photo albums are no big deal. I don't mind you looking through them, especially if it helps us."

"This sort of magic—the kind I'm trying to use—it relies heavily on a person's connection with another," Ramsey said. "I have to dig into that connection at its most fundamental level. Only then can I hope to do what needs to be done."

"Really?" I scrunched my nose. "It seems to me that a garden variety locator spell would do the trick. I mean, I'm sure he's guarded, but how intense could that guarding be? Plus, we just had contact with him. That should make it easier to pick up on his scent, so to speak."

"This isn't about finding him," Ramsey said. "I can find Abram. It would take some elbow grease, and I might have to get a little closer to the rough end of the magical spectrum than I would like, but now that he's back in the city, pinpointing his location isn't impossible. What I'm trying to do is find the *real* him."

"What?" I swallowed hard and stood instinctively. I set my fork down, allowing the bitter tomato sauce to stain the napkin next to my plate. "You're talking about actually bringing him back?"

"I am," Ramsey said flatly. "That's the only way to get to the bottom of all this."

"You told me that was impossible." I narrowed my eyes, trying to not let feelings of betrayal cloud my ability to process our conversation. We all knew that I was hotheaded on a good day. This was definitely not a good day. "You stood there, dead-eyed in the alley, and explained to me that the Abram I would be dealing with wouldn't be the person I knew. You told me he would very likely want me dead. You told me that he'd try to kill me if he could, just to keep me away from him."

"Wanting and having are two very different things, Charisse," Huntsman answered with a grimace. He adjusted one of the tiramisu plates slightly on the counter, a side effect of his compulsion for things to be perfect. "If he comes near you with malice in his heart, it will be the last thing he ever does."

The idea of a no holds barred battle between Huntsman and the new Abram struck me as the worst of all possible outcomes. It was a situation where, literally, no one could win. One of them would end up dead, and the winner would most likely follow shortly after. They were too evenly matched. Still, it meant something that the man thought highly enough of me to throw down a gauntlet like that, and mean it with every bit of his being.

"I told you those things because, in all likelihood, they're true," Ramsey said. "The magic I'm pulling at is dark and dangerous, which is why I felt the need to make you aware of the risks. Even with a ton of skill and some hope, the magic is volatile; the chances of Abram coming back exactly the way you knew him are not good. Still, it's worth a try, if you are willing to take the chance and agree with what I want to do."

"If I agree?" I scoffed. "Is that a joke? If so, it's not very funny. Of course I agree with whatever you have cooking in that brain of yours. It's literally the only thing I've wanted since the moment Abram left and you told me I could never get him back." Reading the concerned look on Ramsey's face, I shook my head. "Before you even ask: yes, I heard you. I know the likelihood is crappy, but a long shot with a tiny chance of success is better than none at all." I steadied myself. "I'll take what I can get."

"Okay, then," Ramsey said, setting his own fork down much neater next to his plate than I'd set mine. "In that case, I need to warn you that, in order to connect with the Abram that he used to be, I'll have to dive deep into your subconscious. I'll have to get at your memories of the man and use them to find a semblance of the psyche he used to have. Assuming it's in there somewhere and the shards of it aren't too broken, I can rebuild his psyche using your memories to fill in the gaps."

"And what of her?" Huntsman asked, his jaw a rigid line of worry. "What sort of dangers does Charisse face because of this procedure?"

"I don't care about the danger," I said instinctively, my hands firming into fists at my sides. "Just do it."

"As brave and selfless as that might seem, there are more people to consider, Charisse," Huntsman said. "This is all happening because of me, and I won't have one of the finest people I've ever met meet her end just to save a life that, some say, should have ended long ago."

"Who would ever say that about you?" I asked, looking at Huntsman with nothing but love and respect.

"More people than you would think." Huntsman leaned his forearms on the counter and stared across the way at me. "I have made many enemies in my lifetime, Charisse. Even those who do not hate me might believe I have lived long enough." He averted his gaze toward a window above the kitchen sink. "Perhaps I believe that as well."

I watched as the truth filtered through his being. Huntsman was giving up, and he expected me to sit back and just be okay with his decision. Well, I wasn't.

"Too bad," I said, getting angrier by the second. "None of us get to choose when we die, Huntsman. That's not the way it works. You might be tired. Lord knows, I can understand that. The truth is, there's still more work to do for both of us. Besides, what you would be facing isn't death. It's something much worse. So, with all due respect to your chivalry and whatever other outdated nonsense you're about to throw my way, the truth is, it's my life, and I'll risk it anytime I damn well please." I nodded at the man, slightly out of breath. "Is that clear?"

My chest was heaving, and they were both looking at me with a sense of fear and admiration.

Huntsman smiled a little as he pushed away from the counter and drummed his hands on the ledge. "Women of this age don't exactly wait for princes to come sweep them off their feet, do they?"

"No," I replied. "I much prefer standing on my own, thank you very much."

Turning back to Ramsey, I found him circling the candle in salt. He knew I wasn't going to let Huntsman talk me down, and he was preparing just the same.

"Sit back down," he said without looking at me, passing around the candle with a second circle of the white granules. "The memory of this night, of the date you shared with Abram and the picture of it you stuck in your photo album, will serve as an anchor. Let the memories wash over you. Think about the man you love, about the reasons you love him, and about the things that piss you off, too. We don't want a perfect version of him, Charisse. We want him as he was, everything you both loved and hated about the man. Having the whole picture is the only way that we'll be able to have even a glimmer of hope for this to work."

"Even his ugly bits were sexy," I muttered petulantly, sitting back down with a huff.

"Good," my mage said. "Then it won't be difficult or cumbersome for you to call them to mind."

He threw some sort of sand on the candle, and the flame went from white to pitch black.

"I don't like the look of that," I whispered.

"They're intense magics," he said. "You know that a black flame does not mean darkness or evil. Just brace yourself. The memories could be overwhelming. You might find yourself lost in them."

"Lost in memories of Abram?" I asked. "I can think of a few worse things that could happen."

"Good," Ramsey replied thoughtfully. "Now close your eyes and think of him."

I took a deep, shaky breath as I let my eyelids fall closed and called him to mind, as though he weren't always there.

The vision of him came easily, starting right with the first time I fell into his arms, quite literally. I smiled to myself. I had fallen head over heels *into* him. Right down the stairs to his basement club where he caught me just outside the door, gazed down at me, and murmured something about the freckle in my eye.

He was deviously handsome, even then. He was also the epitome of stubborn, mysterious, old-fashioned, outdated, and too serious for his own good.

That stubbornness and anger turned to fire and passion over time. With him, I found love and happiness in a way I had never thought or expected could happen.

As infuriating as he could be at times, I wouldn't want to change a hair on his head if I were lucky enough to get him back.

He made me feel emotions I didn't even know existed.

I felt the pull of something like sleep. Only, this wasn't sleep. This was something deeper, something darker. This was a true calm, an endless tunnel of nothingness. But it was all right. It was peace. It was tranquility. It was transformative.

"What are you doing?" a voice asked me, light and free.

My eyes flung open, and I was back in the old apartment. The one I'd shared with Abram.

The same dinner sat in front of me, burnt and unappetizing. Across from me, though, sat the man I would give anything for.

Abram looked back at me with kind and fiery eyes. *His* eyes. The eyes I craved with every fiber of my being.

"What's the matter?" he asked, the edges of his mouth crooking up into a smile. "You look as if you've seen a ghost." His voice held that same accent, the one he'd been missing in the abandoned building earlier.

"You," I whispered. "You're here." I reached out to touch him, and when my fingers met his skin, I almost fainted.

CHAPTER 10

I STARED AT ABRAM, the creases of his mouth, the crinkles on his forehead, the pores on his face. It was all him, right down to the last hair, right down to the last freckle. I was actually sitting here, in front of him.

Better than the fact that he looked like himself, was that he actually *was* himself. This wasn't some sort of damaged, carbon-copy of the greatest man I'd ever known. This was him, plain and simple. This was the real deal, the original Abram. The man I'd love for the rest of my life, no matter where he was.

"You're here," I said lovingly as he reached over with his other hand and stroked my fingers with his.

Squeezing, he said, "Of course, I'm here. You called for me, didn't you?"

I blinked, remembering the memory of the night I was in and wondering if, by some bizarre method, I had actually managed to travel back in time. Lord knows, it wouldn't have been the strangest thing I had ever been through. At this point, time travel just seemed like another check to tick off my bucket list.

This moment certainly *felt* real. My mind started racing

with the possibilities. If that were the case, maybe I could change things altogether. Maybe it meant I could warn Abram of what the future was going to hold and save him from the horrible fate that was about to befall us both.

As fast as the hope filled my chest, it left. Maybe if I said something to him, it would break the memory and I'd be right back in the present, without his essence.

I knew better than that. That was the easy way out. The coward's way. Nothing had ever been that easy for me.

I had been through enough to know that, even if I were actually in the past, redirecting the flow of history would only serve to open us up to a whole host of new issues. At this point, we still hadn't saved Briar. We still hadn't defeated Mandrake and freed Charlie Prince. What if, in an effort to change what was to come, I doomed both of them, and us? What if I made everything so much worse? What if I couldn't do anything for any of them and it destroyed all of us?

Though I hated the fact that Abram was gone, I couldn't deny that being on my own had given me a strength I never knew was possible. It had made me fiercer and more dangerous than I'd ever be with Abram. I would need those qualities if I was going to stand even the slightest chance at taking down The Brothers, with or without Abram at my side.

So, yeah, it sucked, but I was going to have to let this one ride out. Because even if I wanted to change the past, there was nothing I could do that wouldn't have a shattering effect on the world around us.

As he took my hand again, grazing my knuckles with his smooth lips, I realized I could have chosen a lot worse memories to come back to.

My mind reeled ahead to what happened next. In fact, I thought about it often. Things were about to get really fun, and it had been so long for me. I think I needed the excitement of what was coming.

"You're the most beautiful thing I've ever seen," Abram

said, looking up at me with eyes that were a mixture of awe and raw, passionate hunger.

"Good," I said, standing and pulling my hand free.

A shocked look of pleasure crossed his face. The first time this night happened, Abram took the lead. It was great, one of the best nights of my life, actually. Still, I wasn't the woman I'd been back then. Now I knew what I wanted, and thankfully, I was woman enough to take it.

After sliding off the shoulders of my white dress, I let it slip it down to my feet, then stepped out of it, leaving it in a heap of fabric on the floor. Since the damn thing was too tight for either underwear or a bra, I was left completely naked, save for my pearls and heels.

Abram's eyes widened, and the features on his face intensified with his white hot desire for me. I had forgotten about that, just how animalistic my man could get when I turned him on. It was like the beast, the monster that lived inside of him, was sitting just under the surface. One wrong move, and he would tear my throat out. One right move, and he'd make me glad I was a woman.

"What are you doing?" he asked, his Adam's apple bobbing as he forced his gaze from my curves to my face. "We haven't even eaten yet."

Judging by the expression on his face, there was no way Abram actually cared about the food right now.

"That food is a disaster," I answered, like I'd wanted to tell him the first time this happened. "You'll choke it down, of course, and you'll pretend it's not disgusting. You're good like that. The truth is, though, neither of us came here for food." I cocked my naked hip to the side and winked. He turned me into a hussy, and I loved every second of it. "You and me, we're always here for something else. Something better than food could ever be."

I rounded the table, my heels tapping steadily against the kitchen tile. As I passed him, I let my fingers drag across his arm, up to his shoulder, and then walked my fingers up his neck, the way I knew he loved to be touched. His yearning radiated off his skin, and my body perked up in response.

"So," I said, in my best and flirtiest tone, "I'm going to give you a choice. You can either stay here and pretend to enjoy my spaghetti, or you can follow me into the bedroom and I'll give you something I'm sure you'll enjoy a lot mo—"

Before I could finish the sentence, I was grabbed up from behind.

I'd almost forgotten how fast he was. Faster than any man had the right to be, that was for sure.

The world was a whirl, and by the time it stopped, I was on the bed, breathless. Abram was shirtless in front of me and his pants had already been unbuttoned. He bit his lower lip as he breathed, and it was enough to make my nipples go hard and every part of my body clutch with need.

He pinned me with his gaze. "I'm going to—"

I sat up on my heels, the mattress sinking beneath me, and pressed my finger over his lips. "This isn't about what you're going to do to me, Abram. This is about what *I'm* going to do to *you*."

Moving my finger from his mouth, I put both hands on the sides of his pants and pulled them down with a hard tug. In one instant, he was exposed in front of me, the full mast of his passion jutting upward, and he wasn't the slightest bit ashamed. That was another region where I'd forgotten about just how impressive he was.

I let go of his pants and put my hands on the bed beside me, the cotton sheets cool against my palm. Magic flew from my fingertips. It lifted him, spun him around, and tossed him onto the bed. His eyes widened and his eyebrows pulled together all at once. He'd never seen me with that much control of my magic.

Of course. Because, to him, this was coming out of nowhere and so unlike me. Unlike the me he knew when this memory took place. The last time this night happened, I was neither this forward nor this powerful. That didn't matter, though. He seemed to enjoy it, which meant he was really going to enjoy what happened next.

Casting the smallest of spells on my fingertips, I made it so that everywhere I touched on the man would become an erogenous zone. Regardless of where my fingertips fell, Abram would feel more and more. He would get fuller and fuller, harder and harder, until finally he would burst in the most amazing way possible.

Climbing on top of him, I allowed my fingers to graze his legs.

"What?" He gasped, his entire body clenching. "What did you—"

"Just enjoy it," I said, running my other hand up his leg and onto his abs. He jerked, his entire being shuddering with the contact.

Abram groaned beneath me, so low it was almost a growl. His hands slid along my thighs, over my hips, and up my sides until he reached my breasts. The intensity in his gaze sent a ripple of pleasure through my body as his thumbs rubbed across my nipples.

Abram didn't need to use magic to turn me on. He *was* magic. Every inch of his body was made for mine and my pleasure.

Beneath me, his cock pressed against the underside of my thigh, and I lifted up to grab it gently and guide him to where we both needed him to be. He was so swollen with desire that his girth became just a little too much to slide in easily. He moaned as he nudged against me, pushing in the tip and seemingly watching my expression to make sure I wasn't in any pain. Just like he always did.

His thumbs rubbed against my nipples again, sending another shock of pleasure to my core as he pressed more, stretching me to get deeper.

I moaned, sliding down on him farther, determined that, this time, *I* would be the one to drive *him* crazy.

I missed his hands, his touch. I missed the way our bodies seems to crash together so perfectly. How fulfilled I felt in every way being around him.

As I started to grind against his body, his passion intensified. His teasing grazes against my nipple turned into light pinches. He moved one of his hands to my mouth, tracing his finger across my lip. I rolled my tongue around his finger and sucked, my mind flooding back to the memory of the blow job I'd given him back in New Haven.

Hunger flooded him anew, and his thrusts rose to match mine. He sat up and flipped me onto my back, grabbed my wrists, and pinned them over my head, growling. I should have expected it from him, and I nearly giggled.

He slowed down his thrusts to a teasing torture and dropped his lips to my neck, my collarbone, my nipples, taking his time until I was whimpering for more before he drove deeper into me.

Abram wasn't some man disillusioned by internet sex; he knew how to make a women feel good. Knew how to grind his pelvis against that perfect spot as he filled me in ways I didn't think were possible. He found that perfect stride that made me tense and moan until finally sending me over the edge, making me shudder on the edge of explosion.

As he released inside of me, I shattered. The first orgasm I'd felt from another person in a year rolled through my body and left me exhausted. I had never felt more alive, never felt more joined to another person in my life. I was with Abram. I was happy and free.

Maybe I could just stay here, in this moment. Forever. As I tried to think about how I could make it happen, I knew I was being stupid. There was no way that it could be.

I opened my eyes, spent and satisfied in the best way imaginable...until I felt the pull of the emptiness again.

Everything around me fading until I was aware that it was only a memory. A shadow of one of the best nights in my entire life.

Just as quickly as I'd let myself get caught up in the memory, a cold dose of reality washed over me. None of this was actually in my control. It never had been. I was a pawn, a piece that had to be moved at exactly the right time, making it the right sacrifice for some bigger plan. Now, right now, it was time for me to take my leave. To get back to the real world, the current timeline. The place where everything sucked.

I had to do that, though, if I ever wanted a chance at what I'd just experienced to be *real* again.

I sighed, looking up at Abram, who was gazing down at me with a heady, half-lidded stare. After a moment, he dropped onto the bed beside me, his messy hair crushing in every direction against a flat white pillow.

Before I left, there were things I needed to tell him. Things that might not help anything, but that I needed to say for my sake, in case I would never actually see or speak to the real Abram again.

I needed to put a bookend on this in the event that this was the last chance I'd ever have.

The thought struck me like a blow to the chest. Suddenly I wanted to soak in every moment that I had. The soft orange glow of the bedside lamp light. The emerald green suede chair in the corner of the room and the rose wallpaper on the wall behind the bed. Our heavy duty bed-frame that looked so bulky in the otherwise feminine room, and the cheesy popcorn spray ceiling collecting dust that all the apartments in our area were known for. Everything around me that I'd taken for granted during the time that we had.

The twill of Abram's dark-wash jeans. Abram's shaded jaw, his dark eyes and hair, his tanned skin. His musky, sandalwood scent, the thick dark hair on his arms. His full lips, and that energy that was always buzzing beneath the surface whenever I was around him.

I didn't want to forget a single detail. But I was running out of time to soak it all in. I could feel the present calling me back from the past, and I didn't know how many more seconds I had of this happiness before it was all taken away from me.

"I love you," I said frantically, rushing the words out.

I sat up, not even bothering to pull the comforter from the bottom of the bed to cover my body. That's something old Charisse would have done. Something I might have still done, if I were going to say here. But I wasn't. It didn't matter that I wasn't ashamed of my curves, I was still pretty shy about my body.

"You are the love of my life," I continued, "and if everything goes to hell tomorrow, I want you to know I don't regret a single second. If I could do it all over again, if I could take the ride just to take the fall, I would a thousand times. That's how much you mean to me."

"Charisse," Abram said, sitting up to face me, his eyebrows pulling together. "What are you talking about? I love you, too, but there's not going to be any fall. I would never let anything happen to you. I would never let anything happen to us. There is too much meant for us in this life. Nothing will ever come between us."

In that moment, I believed him. Even though I knew better, even though I knew the way it was all going to turn out, I believed him. That's how powerful he was, how powerful he'd always been.

"Just try to remember me," I said, fighting back sobs that I hadn't realized were there waiting on the edge of my mind. "Do your best. Try to remember me, no matter what happens."

"Always, my love," he said soothingly. "Always."

As Abram spoke, the darkness took me, swallowing me

whole and leaving nothing behind. I tried to fight it with everything I had in me, but my everything wasn't enough. It pulled me deep and then spit me out back where I was in the first place.

Except when I arrived on the "other side," things had changed. The table I was sitting at had been cleared of food, and the fading sun had been replaced by the night sky shining brightly through the windows.

Ramsey was sitting in front of me, his eyes heavy and his hair a mess while he stared at me.

"What?" I croaked, my throat dry and cracking. "What happened?"

My head was pounding, and I couldn't stop shaking.

"It's Abram," Ramsey said softly, looking up at me. "Something's wrong."

CHAPTER 11

RAMSEY'S WORDS brought me to my knees. *It's Abram. Something's wrong.*

The moment of pleasure I had just experienced in his arms was shattered by this harsh revelation. Being sucked back into this world—this dark and twisted Abram-free place —would have been hard enough. Knowing that something was wrong, knowing that the spell Ramsey had cast using my Supplicant blood and powered by my Conduit magic, had backfired… It was enough to send me running for the hills, or the blankets on my bed that I could cuddle up in and pretend nothing was wrong.

"Do you need some water?" Ramsey asked, exhaustion coloring both his face and his voice.

One look at him was enough to tell me that, while I had been having the time of my life, Ramsey had been going through the fight of his. My heart went out to him, but the truth was that I needed more than just something to drink. I needed to know what was going on. I had to know exactly what was going on if I was going to be able to do anything about it. I needed information to make a plan.

I took a deep breath, readying myself for anything but

expecting the worst. More than anything, I wished that I could go back in time, just a few minutes, and kiss Abram one more time.

"What happened?" I asked tentatively. "What happened to ruin the spell? Whatever it is, can we undo it?"

Even speaking was taking its toll, and I felt dizzy with the exertion of rushing those words out. I closed my eyes, hoping to get a little bit of a break from the lights that were spinning, and Ramsey, who wouldn't tell me what I wanted to know.

The idea that this might be the end came popping into my head unexpectedly.

Not the end of my life, no. Worse than that would be the end of everything that I had held onto for the past year. Abram. Our life together. The life he swore we would have, and the one that he gave up his very essence to protect.

I knew I was kidding myself when I'd stayed up late and dreamt of him living a life away from me. Hell, when he'd left me, I knew he was leaving me to die. He was leaving to keep me safe, to keep me away from the magic that was eating at him from the inside out. The magic and darkness that were bound to destroy him. Only now, I was having to face the fact that I might have made it worse.

What if the spell had backfired to such an extent that Abram was dead and gone? What if Ramsey had not only destroyed the pieces of Abram's mind that were left floating in there, but killed his body as well? Would I be able to live with that: a truly Abram-free world?

Knowing that I wouldn't, I leaned forward and started hyperventilating. I couldn't do this.

"I knew you needed water," he chided while shaking his head. "The spell you were just under can be tough, and it wreaks havoc on the body," Ramsey said, while getting up and rushing to the sink.

I stared at him blankly as he fumbled around the kitchen for the glasses. If it were any other time, I could joke and make comments about how he needed to spend more time in the kitchen. Right now, though, I wanted to scream in frustration.

If I wasn't feeling so miserable from being in the pocket dimension and then getting sucked back, I'd get up and force him to pay attention to me. As it was, I wouldn't be able to get him to do much of anything. I'd had a year's worth of experience in trying to get him off his train of thought. It didn't work well. Almost ever.

He turned on the tap and stuck a glass that he'd finally found above the sink under the current as I gathered myself, pushing the sickness down and trying to focus. It was a lot harder than it should have been, and the sound of the sink running made me want to hit Ramsey upside the head with a baseball bat.

"Screw the water, and screw my body!" I snapped when I couldn't take it anymore. "Just tell me what the hell happened to Abram." I slammed my hand down on the table and sat back upright despite the nausea. "I need to know, Ramsey." Blinking hard, I found familiar tears stinging the backs of my eyelids and did my best to keep them in check. "Is he... Did he die? You owe me the truth. Tell me."

Ramsey sighed before turning the water off and taking his ever loving time moving the dozen or so feet between the rooms. I stared at him, venom in my eyes, as he sat down slowly and slid the water across the table.

I growled as he motioned for me to drink. There was a look on his face that told me he would answer my question only after I took care of myself and drank the offered water. Reluctantly, I grabbed the glass and took a gulp.

As much as I hated to admit it, Ramsey was right. The soothing way the liquid slid down my throat told me I was wrong. I needed water. It wasn't until the glass was empty that I let myself acknowledge that he knew what I needed better than I did—at least when it came to the after effects of magic.

Setting the glass on the table, I looked at him and waited. I knew what I looked like. I could feel the muscles in my face pulled back in trepidation. Ramsey stared at me for a few long moments, and it wasn't until I started tapping my fingers on the table that he spoke.

"I wish..." he finally said while eyeing my fingers as if he was afraid I would attack him with magic at any moment. "I wish he had died. That would be easier than the hell he's going to live in for the rest of his life."

I was all at once furious and concerned at that sentiment. What the hell? My heart fell. What on earth did that mean? What would be harder than death?

Who was I kidding? I'd been living an existence worse than death for the past year.

I wasn't about to play guessing games with the man in front of me though, and I wasn't about to let him know I was on the verge of begging at this point. I steeled my gaze and nodded for him to continue, hoping he got the point and just gave me the information I wanted without me having to punch him.

"The spell was going fine at first," he went on as though there hadn't been a long pause. "As I said, it's complicated. There are a lot of intricate neurological pathways in the brain, and when that brain is tainted with and runs on magic, those pathways became literal landmines." Ramsey took a deep breath and ran his hands through his hair, obviously distressed by what had happened. "Still, I was working my way through them. The information I was gleaning from you came in as a stream, just as it was supposed to. I'm not sure what you were doing in your little pocket dimension of your own subconscious, but it worked. I had enough to rebuild him."

"Okay," I said, pushing down a blush as I thought of what I had just done with Abram in that pocket dimension Ramsey mentioned. "All of that sounds good. What happened to screw it up?"

"The landmines," Ramsey said. "Whoever did this to him, whoever took his mind and twisted it into what it was when we ran into him the other day, placed protective measures there." He shook his head. "God help me, I wasn't expecting things to get out of hand like they did. Perhaps I should have, but I didn't."

The man in front of me pretty much fell apart. All of the strength I was used to him carrying faded away, leaving nothing but a desolate and miserable shell where the powerful mage usually stood. Under normal circumstances, I would call Briar to have her make him feel better when something like this happened, but there was no way I was going to bring her into the middle of this craziness. The last thing she needed was to have her life thrown into chaos because of magic. *Again*.

"It's all right," I said instinctively, needing to offer him the same comfort that he'd offered me for the past year. "None of us knew what we were getting ourselves into here."

I awkwardly patted him on the shoulder.

"It's my *job* to know," he snarled, blinking back tears of his own. "It's my job, and I messed up, and now Abram is going to suffer because of it."

"Suffer?" I asked, my heart leaping horribly. "What do you mean?"

My mind was already racing with the possibilities of what could have happened. While I'd been selfishly spending time with him in the pocket dimension, something happened and now he was going to suffer. Self-doubt filled my mind while I impatiently waited for Ramsey to pull himself together.

"When I hit the protective measure," he said, "I'll call it a landmine. It exploded before I could get around it safely." Ramsey looked down at the table, and he fell back into the chair across from me, breaking the connection we'd had while he smothered his face with his hands in frustration. "It sent pieces of what I'd done scattering to the corners of his mind.

All the information you sent me was out of position. A lesser mage wouldn't have been able to do anything with it, and with that intel already inside Abram's mind, there would have been nothing left to do. We couldn't have replaced it there. The duality of such a thing would break his psyche altogether. It would have been over."

"'Would have' means it isn't," I said, mentally chiding myself for the rush of hope that filled my chest, but relishing it nonetheless. "That means you did something to fix it. Or you could do something to fix it."

I sat forward, and even though I wanted to pretend that I had my shit together, I didn't. I needed him to tell me what he'd done.

"Oh, I did something," he admitted, shaking his head. "And I regret it with every tiny piece of my soul."

The desolation in his voice filled me with dread. "What happened, Ramsey?" I swallowed hard, afraid of what I was about to hear.

"I was able to get the pieces before they scattered too far," he said with a self-deprecating smile. "I placed them together, a full copy of Abram's mind, a place for his soul to rest, and I encircled it with your magic. I thought it would be enough to allow him to take over, but the protective measure did more than decimate what I had built. It solidified what the person who did this to Abram did. It made the thing running his brain its default setting. I can't undo it now, and that means that a fully conscious version of Abram is tucked inside of a mind and body he can't control."

"What?" I asked, my chest tightening. I knew the words he was saying, I knew what he was telling me, but my brain wasn't comprehending it. It couldn't be true.

"He's stuck in there, Charisse," Ramsey said. "Like Huntsman with the bottle. He's trapped inside a vessel he can never control or get out of. The only, and I mean *only*, bright spot is that the bastard is strong enough to break free every once in awhile." Ramsey shook his head. "For a few seconds at a time, anyway, once, for almost half an hour while you were in that pocket dimension. During those breakthroughs, he's back to himself. The true Abram takes over. Those moments are fleeting, though. I could tell when he did it that it was causing him excruciating pain."

"My God," I said, horrified.

"I know you already hate me for this, but that's not the last of it," he muttered. "That's not the nail in the coffin on what happened to him. Of what Abram is going through, over and over again."

I looked at him, not understanding what the mage was trying to say to me. "Spit it out. What is it?"

"There's something else," Ramsey said. "It's the way I know he's coming through, and that it's not the replacement tricking me." He looked down at his hands, and all of a sudden our entire conversation came rushing back at me.

The time, the way he kept talking about Abram and how he was able to fix it. Something wasn't adding up, and as much as I wanted to wait, I couldn't.

"Ramsey," I said quietly. "I know that I've been gone for hours, but you're making it seem like there's been days. How long has it been?"

"Char," Ramsey said stiltedly. "I don't know how long it's been. Honestly. I know that I found him, and that he's able to come through. That's all I know. Well, that and the reason I know that Abram is able to break free of his prison."

That wasn't it, though. Ramsey was holding something back. Something more, something so much more powerful and important that I instinctively curled into a ball and held onto my legs for all they were worth. Even though I was afraid and didn't want him to tell me, I needed it.

"What do you mean?" I asked once I was ready to hear the rest.

My heart was beating furiously in my throat. Things

couldn't get much worse than they were right then, but I had to know what was happening. I had to know, or I'd be nothing more than the girl who was afraid to leave New Haven. I couldn't hide from this. I couldn't run from what I'd had a part in doing to Abram.

"Right as the true Abram is managing to take over, he always says the same thing," Ramsey answered. "Before he's sucked back into oblivion."

"What?" I demanded. "What does he say?"

"He says 'Always, my love,'" Ramsey said mournfully. "Always."

CHAPTER 12

WITH MY HEART in my throat and my mind basically in pieces on the floor, I tried to think of anything I could do to avert the disaster that lay in front of me.

The idea of Abram—my Abram—being trapped inside a body he could neither control nor escape was pretty much the worst thing I could imagine. Well, maybe except for death. Still, here we were. Things had gone wrong, as things always seemed to do when they involved me. The worst had not only become a possibility, but also the reality I would have to suffer through.

"He's beyond that door," Huntsman said, sidling up next to me inside the hallway of my apartment building.

"Thanks," I said tonelessly.

Of course, I knew Abram was beyond this door. It was why I was standing here. It was why I had been standing at this door for nearly fifteen minutes now. He was calling to me. From somewhere deep down inside, the Abram that I could never really touch was begging for my help. Okay, so maybe I was imagining that part, but I knew Abram. He would hate being trapped anywhere.

No, Abram would want me to do anything I could to stay

safe. He would be livid that I'd gotten involved at all, and now here I was. Standing here, not moving. No matter what I did, or which way I turned, I was going to change everything.

"Ugh," I groaned.

Huntsman grunted at my side, but he didn't leave. Instead, he let me get absorbed in my own mind, and in return I ignored him completely.

I had every intention of going into that apartment, of looking the man that had taken over Abram's body directly in the eyes in hopes of being able to find a piece of my love in there and figuring a way of pulling him out. I had nothing but good intentions, and still I couldn't move. I was being stupid, though, and I knew it. That's what I was: some stupid girl who believed her love was strong enough to change something even magic could not.

That was why I couldn't muster the courage to go inside. I knew the truth. I knew I would fail, just like the spell had failed in the first place. I knew my hubris had condemned the man I loved to a near endless lifetime of torment, and I wasn't ready to face that. I didn't know if I'd ever be ready to face that, quite honestly.

Nope. Maybe one day when I was more than what I am.

"I can inform you of the next time he's acting like himself, if you'd prefer," Huntsman said, almost sheepishly, as he shuffled beside me. "Perhaps that would be easier for you."

I knew he was there, but in my contemplation, I'd forgotten I wasn't alone.

"You know," I said, scoffing and almost chuckling bitterly at the idea of what I was about to say. "I think that would make it harder, actually. At least this way I can face him without the familiarity in his eyes when I tell him what I've done."

I turned to Huntsman, taking in the weary and even guilty look on his face. Still, I had no tears in my eyes. I had cried enough for one day, it seemed. I'd probably cried enough for a lifetime in the past year, and now it seemed like I was done. Regardless of how upset, how devastated I was, there wasn't even the slightest hint of tears behind my eyes.

"It's weird," I said. "All I've wanted since the second he left was for him to come back to me. Now, I don't know that I can face him even if he's not really there. I think it would be easier to look at the thing that took his place, to look in his eyes and not see my Abram looking back at me." I cleared my throat. "I failed him. Worse than that, I've harmed him, and I don't want to have to sit down next to him and explain the things that I've done while trying to save him."

"Are you sure he'd see it that way?" Huntsman asked, blinking hard. "While I'll admit there were times we didn't always see eye to eye, I found Abram to be a fair person. What's more, I found him to have the capacity to forgive anything, especially when it comes to you. Do you really think he wouldn't forgive you for this?"

"I don't want him to have to forgive me for what I've done," I said defiantly. "I want him to be *with* me. I know Ramsey told me it was a longshot. I know he said the likelihood wasn't in our favor. But the truth was, deep down, I believed it was going to work. I don't know why I believed that."

"I do," Huntsman said, placing a hand on my shoulder. "The two of you have been beating the odds since the moment you met. You've gotten through things that even the stories of old couldn't compete with when it comes to trials of love. It only makes sense to me that, somewhere along the way, at least part of you would begin to believe you were invincible, the exception to all of the rules the rest of the world faces."

"I guess rules like that don't have exceptions," I muttered mournfully, thinking about the past as well as what the future might now hold for all of us, since I'd torn away any chance of redeeming Abram.

"I wouldn't be so sure," he said. "I've watched the two of you before. I've seen you down and out, and I've witnessed you come back from things that would have crippled lesser men, You have left me astounded on more than one occasion." He squeezed my shoulder. "Sometimes, we think we're at the end of our story only to find out it's simply a bump along the road to finding a happy ending."

I looked up at the man, grateful for what he was trying to do, but I knew the truth. Not all stories had happy endings. If that were the case, my mom would have beat her fight with cancer. I swallowed back the tears pinching my throat. That seemed like a lifetime ago now. I knew I wasn't meant to have a happy ending. Everything I touched was cursed.

"I'm not sure that's something I would expect to hear coming from a warrior's mouth," I said, deflecting from what I was really feeling and doing my best to get a handle on the emotions simmering under the surface.

"I suppose this warrior has changed, Charisse Bellamy," he answered softly, and I could practically feel the weight on him as his shoulders slumped down.

"I'm sorry," I said, shaking my head and kicking myself for being so damn self-centered.

While I was going through my own crap, I had completely forgotten that Huntsman had his own issues to deal with. Like the fact that we currently had less than three days to help him get out of being stuck in a lamp for the foreseeable future.

"Don't be sorry for me Charisse Bellamy," he said. "It's perfectly reasonable to think of those closest to your heart first."

"You're close to my heart, too," I said honestly. "I'd have been dead a hundred times over if not for you."

"Then, I guess that makes the both of us warriors," he answered plainly.

"We're going to find a way to get you out of this," I said, motioning back away from both of us. "Even now, Ramsey is working on a spell to find that damn genie. We might not have Abram back in the way I want him, but he's here nonetheless. We have access to his powers, and that means we can use them to get to this genie, maybe even force her back into that bottle."

"To what end?" Huntsman asked, surprising me so much that my mouth dropped open.

"To the end of you not spending all of eternity trapped in some brass prison. I thought that much was clear."

"But she will, right? The genie?" he asked, and I could see the pain as it flashed across his perfect features. "She'll be trapped in there again."

"I think that's the way it works," I said, narrowing my eyes as I tried to decipher what he was getting at. "Are you saying you don't want her to have to do that?"

It would be just like Huntsman, though. To have feelings and regret for giving the curse back to the one who gave it to him in the first place.

"If I am a victim in this, then it only makes sense that she is, too," he said logically. "Who knows what sort of devious djinn trapped her in there and how long she was actually suffering before she was released?" His words brought forth a vision of torment and curses, much like the one Abram had been forced to endure for a lifetime before he met me.

"Yes," I said, nodding. "All of that's very sad, but it's no reason to throw yourself on a sword for someone you hardly know."

"Isn't that what you're doing?" Huntsman challenged.

I looked back at the door that stood between me and the man who used to be Abram. "That's not the same, and you know it," I said, a spike of anger rising in me that I was useless to quell. "That might not technically be the Abram I knew, but he is still Abram." I pointed at the door, unable to help myself or the temper tantrum I'd started. "That's the person I love."

"Of course he is," Huntsman soothed without even a hint of sarcasm. "But he's not who I'm talking about."

"What?" I balked. "If not him, then who?"

"The men, women, and children you see walking along on the sidewalk," he said. "The person out there working in the deli down the street, or the people you find selling pirated mixed tapes out of the trunk of their car in a mall parking lot. And whoever else you've spent these last months trying to protect without them knowing the sacrifice or danger you're facing."

"I'm almost for certain mixed tapes aren't a thing anymore," I said, ignoring the rest of the sense he was making. "At least, not to the point that you could make a living selling them out of your car."

"Really?" Huntsman mused. "I thought those were here to stay. It doesn't matter," he said with a shrug. "The point is, you're willing to sacrifice yourself for the world at large, filled to the brim with people you'll never know. You're giving your whole life away for it."

"The Brothers are after me anyway," I said, spreading my hands. "What am I supposed to do? Lay down and take whatever they're throwing at me? Not only that, but the people out there don't deserve the chaos and destruction that rains down on them on a daily basis. I have the power to stop it."

"You don't think The Brothers would stop if you allowed them to bind your powers and signed a blood oath swearing to never interfere in their business?" Huntsman asked with a pointed look. "You're a smart girl, Charisse. You know what you're doing, and why you're doing it. You chose to help because it's your nature. How is that any different than what I'm talking about?"

I took a deep breath, trying to steady myself but failing epically. "It's different because, with me, the whole damn world is at stake!" I seethed at him. "Not one little life."

"The whole world is more important to you than a singular life?" Huntsman asked. "To this genie, her life is the whole world. Who am I to take that away from her if given the chance?"

"Are you serious with this garbage right now?" I sighed, shaking my head in disbelief. "I just went through hell for this, Huntsman. I just broke the brain of the only man I've ever loved to find a way to get you out of this, and now you're telling me you don't even want to try."

"That's not what I'm saying," he backtracked quickly. "I'm just saying that maybe this is my destiny. Maybe I was brought here, to her, to pick up the mantle where she laid it to rest. Maybe it's for me to bring her peace."

"And what about your own peace?" I asked. "Because if you do this, you don't get it. Ever. You won't ever pick that axe up again, but you don't get to lay it down, either. You don't get to rest. You get endless torment while a world that could really use a guy like you has to suffer through the worst part of its history without you."

I grabbed his hand and pleaded with him. "I know this is hard, and it goes against your nature, but you deserve to be happy, too. You deserve to rest at some point. I know this girl is a victim here, along with you. I get that, and it sucks. I can only put out the fires in front of me, and right now, the most important fire I see is the one blazing around *you*."

Huntsman shook his head at me like I was a pitiful child that needed to be reminded of something important. "If I had the power of a djinn, I could bring him back to you," he said quickly, glancing toward the door and cutting me to the core. "I could bring him back and hide you from the Brothers. I would never grant your third wish. So, you wouldn't have to worry about being discarded to the bottle, but I could bring you peace. I could allow the fight to move on to the next generation. I could give you everything you wanted, and maybe that would be enough. Maybe that would be a fitting enough end to make all of it worth it."

With every ounce of my being, I wanted to accept his offer. I blinked hard, allowing the picture Huntsman had just painted for me to flash before my eyes before I batted it away with a blink of the eye.

"Stop it," I hissed firmly. "Just stop it. This isn't the end. You told me that yourself. This is just a speed bump, remember? On the way to you finding your own happily ever after."

I stared down the door, anger boiling up from somewhere deep in my gut. I used every bit of that anger to propel me forward. I twisted the handle on the apartment door and pushed it open. Then, before I could chicken out like I wanted to, I stepped over the threshold to face Abram...and whatever the future held.

CHAPTER 13

As I WALKED through the door that led to my past and future all rolled into one, my mind was racing. Leave it to future generations? Didn't Huntsman understand? They were who I was fighting for. I fought today so that the children of tomorrow wouldn't have to. At least, that was my hope going into all of this craziness.

Abram was tucked away in a guest room of sorts. Since I never had any guests, I hadn't seen the need in fancying it up at all. I'd used it for storage in the past, tossing whatever I didn't want to throw away into it and organizing only as necessary. Somewhere in there was a bed, too. As I entered the room, an eerie sense of calm washed over me.

I was dreading this moment, but now, riding high on the wave of my indignation directed at Huntsman, the hesitation pretty much melted away. That, and the fact that I literally couldn't back out now.

I had seen what feeling guilty would get me. Huntsman was willing to toss his entire future away on some misguided notion of helping a woman who very likely didn't deserve it. I wouldn't allow that to happen to myself. I had a job to do.

I had *so many* jobs to do, actually. Plus, if I wanted to start complaining about things, I could go on and on. My life had changed so much, and none of what was happening was anything that I could handle on a regular basis. Now, adding in everything else, I wanted to scream into a pillow. I couldn't, though. Not when I had all of these things that I had to do.

Huntsman was right when he told me the fate of the world rested singularly with me. He did an amazing job and laid the idea of a peaceful and happy existence with the man I loved at my feet. All I had to do was sacrifice Huntsman, as he was so willing for me to do, along with any hope of saving the world.

I didn't even have to think twice before eliminating it completely. Once I had myself composed as well as I could possibly be at that moment, I knocked lightly on the door that led me to Abram, and then I opened it.

Abram was sitting on the twin bed, his legs over the side and feet planted firmly on the ground. Because Abram was such a big man, his knees bent up a little higher than the edge of the mattress as he looked up at the ceiling with his fingers laced together. Beside him, sitting on a pitiful nightstand, was one of those little succulent plants that didn't require a lot of sun or water, and that was pretty much it.

"You know, this place is practically falling apart," he remarked before turning his attention to me and placing me under a microscope.

I could tell from the look on his face, as well as the way he eyed me, that my Abram wasn't in control right now. His eyes were dull, sliced through with a cold, calculating gleam. Gone was the heat. The spark. The genuinity. No, this wasn't the real Abram. I was dealing with the *other* one—the one who would just as soon see me dead. As an afterthought, I realized his accent was back.

I steeled myself, ready for the experience.

"You should really get someone to look at the structural integrity of the roof," he continued. "I'm not comfortable with it."

"Well, if you're not comfortable, then I'll be sure to make it my highest priority," I snapped.

Fake Abram wasn't getting the jump on me this time. This wouldn't be like back in the abandoned building. I wasn't going to let my heart cloud my judgement. At least, no more than I could help. I knew this man was an imposter, and I was going to treat him like one.

For his part, the faux Abram seemed delighted that I was finally sparring with him a little. His face lit up, revealing the smile that had taken my breath away more times than I could have counted. I slapped that sensation down and glared at him with a what I hoped was a look icy enough to freeze him in his twisted mental tracks.

"Maybe you could just loosen the magical bindings holding me here," he suggested lightly, standing to meet me. "Then I could do the work myself. Or, you know, other things."

I didn't miss the way his tongue flicked out across his lip.

"I'm afraid you'll have to take that up with the landlord," I shot back with a nonchalant shrug. "In the meantime, how about we have a little chat?" Just for good measure, I batted my eyelashes to make him think I was stupid enough to think he really was attracted to me and not just trying to get out of the spell's hold.

"Talking really isn't my strong suit," he countered. "But, judging by the way you seemed to miss me the first time we met, I'm betting there are a few other things I could do with my mouth that would fall squarely into my skill set."

Then he had the audacity to wink at me.

My face reddened, a mixture of anger and embarrassment that he'd seen through me. "Shut up before I shut you up," I said. "This isn't playtime. I wouldn't have brought you here if I didn't have to, if it wasn't absolutely necessary. We have a situation, and like it or not, you *are* going to help us with it. Do you understand?"

"I understand that you're making a lot of demands for someone who doesn't have many cards to play. Or really any cards at all for that matter," he quipped almost jokingly as he walked toward me and flexed his power against the spell that was keeping him from killing me where I stood.

"Is that right?" I narrowed my eyes and fought the urge to stick my tongue out at him. "Seeing as how you're our prisoner, I'd say I have more cards than you think I do."

"Doubtful," he sneered. "I saw the way you looked at me. I see the way you're looking at me now, even if you're trying to hide it. You won't do anything to hurt me. You don't have it in you. So, how about you do us both a favor, stop wasting my time, and just let me out of here. We both know that's how this is going to end anyway."

Upon hearing Abram's words, a hundred thoughts flooded through my mind at once. I was angry, of course. I was sad, and upset. I felt guilty and nostalgic. What I wanted more than anything, though, was to make it right. To find a way to take all of this away and put it back to normal.

But I couldn't.

The problem staring me right in the face, at least for the moment, was too big for me. I didn't know how to approach it, even if I wanted to. Which I didn't. Not with a ten foot pole that could protect me. Besides, I had other issues that were drawing my focus. Huntsman's life was on the line, leaving the world with one less person to protect it. I needed to keep my directive clear so I could execute my plan. Abram had taught me that.

Closing my hand into a fist, I mustered up some magic and flung it at Abram. It knocked him off his feet and slammed him hard on his back against the floor. It was something I would never have been able to do if he had all his power. I did it just so he knew I wasn't screwing around. My magic snapped his left arm, a clean break that would hurt like hell, but would heal in time.

"Jesus!" he snarled, looking up at me with an enraged face and a half beast-turned mouth. Fangs jutted out from his lips, reminding me of the beast that always lived under the surface.

For one second, less than that actually, I thought I might have my Abram back. But then I saw the blank expression in his eyes, and I knew it hadn't happened. This Abram was injured, yes, but the physical pain hadn't been enough to buy him time. Rage flooded through me, and I couldn't help letting it pour out of me and into him.

"I think you'll be surprised at what I have in me, *imposter*." I stepped toward him and secured my spell while twitching my fingers. He wouldn't be able to get off the floor now, no matter how hard he tried. Not until I allowed it. At least, that's the way the magic was supposed to work. I had no doubt that the training Ramsey had put me through was about to come in handy. After all, I'd spent hours stuck while trying to figure out how to break the spell.

"You're a crazy bitch!" he howled, writhing in pain. "You want my help, right? How the hell am I supposed to give it to you with a broken arm?" He clenched his jaw and tried to bite back another howl, but I could tell he was struggling. I almost giggled.

"Beasts heal fast," I said by way of explanation. I stepped closer to him and crossed my arms as I glared down at the man that haunted my every waking moment. "Let me make one thing clear before we continue: you don't have any power over me. The man I loved, he's not you. You're not even close. He's gone and won't be coming back. I get that."

I was lying, of course. I knew the true Abram was in there somewhere. I knew he could, very likely, see and hear me right now. At least, I hoped so. Of course, I also knew—thanks to Ramsey—that the Abram in control most of the time didn't seem to know anything about the fractured nature of his brain. He had no memory of what happened when my Abram took over. I could use that knowledge to my advantage, and it would be one of my most powerful weapons against him.

"It took me a long time to come to that conclusion," I continued without missing a beat. "Letting myself accept that Abram was gone was the hardest thing I'd ever had to do, no doubt it is the hardest thing I ever *will* do. It was even harder after seeing you, walking around in his skin. But now, watching you lay on the floor, pathetic and completely unable to defend yourself, I know my Abram is never coming back. He would never, not in a thousand lifetimes, allow this to happen to himself. He was so much more of a man than that."

"You ridiculous cow!" Fake Abram snarled.

"Quiet! I'm talking!" I yelled. With another twist of my hand, Abram's mouth shut. Like his body, it wouldn't move again until I allowed it. "Now, I understand this might be hard for you to grasp. In addition to being more pathetic, you seem stupider than my Abram, too. Still, you're going to have to give it the old college try. It'll be important moving forward that you understand me." I clenched my jaw. "I'm in charge here. Not Ramsey, not the man with the axe you saw earlier, and certainly not you. This is my show. I'm the one who runs it, and I say what goes."

The imposter in Abram's body glared at me.

"Now, you're going to do as I say, or I'm going to rip you into bloody pieces and scatter those pieces to the winds. Is that understood, or do I need to break your other arm to prove to you how serious I am?"

I twisted my hand, allowing him control of his lips again.

"What do you want from me?" he asked, then took a deep breath as he bit down on his lower lip to keep me from seeing how hurt he was.

"A lot of things," I said honestly. "Like I said, we have a problem. The first thing I want from you, though, is to tell me how you got like this and what you've been doing this past year."

"I don't know," he answered in a low, still threatening voice.

I put magical pressure on his broken arm, eliciting another howl. "Don't lie to me," I said lowly. "You won't know what pain is if you lie to me."

"I'm not lying." His harsh gaze drove into my own. "And it hasn't been a year. It's been a couple of months, three tops. I woke up in a back alley in Tijuana, naked as a fucking jaybird. I don't remember anything before that. All I knew was that I was stronger than most people, and that I needed to eat. So, I found the biggest, baddest son of a bitch in town, and I beat the hell out of him. Then, I offered my services to anyone who needed a little assistance. It wasn't long before I was up to my eyeballs in jobs. Pretty soon, I could name my own price. I started selling my services to the highest bidder, and more often than not, that meant people looking for powerful items."

"And you didn't care?" I asked, disgusted. "It didn't matter what kind of person you were giving those items to?"

"As long as their money was right, I was all about it. A man's gotta eat, you know," he said. "You should be thanking me! Your lover's body would have starved otherwise. Besides, what business is it of mine? I don't care what they do. I'm going to be just fine, thanks to my little friend."

"Little friend?" I asked, my eyebrows dancing upward.

"The marking on my chest," he answered. "The source of my powers."

I narrowed my eyes. A flick of the wrist tore Abram's shirt off. Along with an achingly familiar physique, I saw an unfamiliar branding on him. It was an eye, and it had been burned right into his chest, right in the place above his heart.

"That's not the source of your powers," I muttered in confusion. "In fact, I'm not sure what that is."

"What?" Abram asked, his eyes widening as he looked

toward me and a dawning understanding took over his features.

"Don't move," I said, then I laughed to myself, remembering the spell keeping him in place. "Not that you could if you wanted to."

My mind was racing with the possibilities of what was going to happen, and I couldn't pinpoint the worst. None of this could be good for Abram, my Abram. What the imposter had said was ringing in my head. He'd only been conscious for the past few months. That left so much time unaccounted for, that I didn't know what to do. I did, however, know what had to be done.

As I turned toward the door, he called after me with alarm in his voice, "Where are you going?"

"To get to the bottom of this," I answered over my shoulder. "Right now."

CHAPTER 14

RAMSEY PACED the length of the living room, his leather shoes pressing down the fibers of the carpet with each step before they sprang back up again. But it was the looks he kept shooting me—not his pacing habit—that sent my stomach to cartwheels.

At this point, I knew the mage almost as well as I knew myself. I knew the way he looked when he had things under control...and I knew the way he looked when he had just discovered we were fucked six ways from Sunday.

This was beyond the worst six-ways-from-Sunday look I had ever seen come from him. Which was saying something, because in the past year, I'd seen him almost kissed by a Banshee and get his soul sucked out. So, seeing him like this was frightening to say the least.

"This isn't good," he said as he turned on his heel again, pacing toward me now.

"It's a stupid mark, Ramsey," I said dumbly, shaking my head. "What the hell could it possibly matter anyway? Abram thinks it's the source of his powers. I mean, he's wrong, but that doesn't mean it actually has anything to do with what happened to him."

"Except it does," Ramsey explained as he ran his fingers through his hair. "Haven't you learned by now that everything means something, Charisse?" He swallowed hard and settled his gaze on me. "I've seen that mark once before, just once. On the day I saw it, I almost died. I'll never forget it for as long as I live."

I narrowed my eyes. "So, you think this is a curse?"

"I think it's a promise." He turned to pace away from me. "What you're looking at, the mark that has been stamped on Abram's chest...it's a stamp of ownership."

"Ownership?" I asked, bile rising in my throat. "Are you saying that someone bought and sold Abram like he was cattle and then branded him like an animal?"

Ramsey sighed loudly, throwing his hands out to the side as he pivoted again. "That, or he gave himself the mark willingly."

"Why would he do that?"

"Who knows, Charisse." Ramsey shrugged. "Maybe he thought it would suppress whatever magical nature that sent him running away in the first place. Maybe he made a deal with some supernatural being. Either way, we're in deep shit. The mark on his chest comes from an organization called the Tellers. They're a group of powerful mystics, oracles, and the like. You've heard of the Illuminati?" Ramsey stopped rambling, and I realized that he wanted me to answer him.

I balked. "They're the Illuminati?"

I'd grown up hearing stories about the all-powerful organization that had built and destroyed political parties, and even countries, for generations. Only the most powerful people knew of their true existence. Even fewer knew of the power that they could wield or the real extent of their influence.

"No," Ramsey said, stopping in front of me.

When it looked like he was done stalking around the

room, he sat on the couch beside me and rested his elbows on his knees.

"Oh," I said with a sigh of relief.

Ramsey quickly disabused me of that relief, however. "They're the organization that destroyed the Illuminati and built themselves on the ashes that were left smouldering. You have to understand, Charisse, when people have access not only to magic but also to the future itself, they're often tempted to use those abilities to shape the world the way they see fit. Not only are they tempted, but they do it."

Great. Here we go again. More layers. More bad guys. More *problems*. I wanted to scream and throw my hands in the air and rage about how unfair everything was. Every time I thought I had a handle on the monsters we were up against, I was thrown for a loop by another big bad guy showing up.

"The Tellers see themselves as benevolent forces," Ramsey continued through my unspoken objections. "There are even those who speak of them as though they're heroes, meant to be worshipped. They shape the world the way they want. They tell the stories the way they see fit. Even The Brothers leave them alone for the most part. They get what they want. Apparently, what they want is Abram."

"Well, they can't have him," I snapped before I could stop myself. I stared down at my hands as I dug my short, painted nails into my palms and tried to block out the pain. "Especially now, especially since the real Abram is trapped in there somewhere just waiting for me to get him out. These Tellers will just have to learn to live with disappointment, like I have for the past year."

Even as I said the words, though, I knew I was about to find out it was impossible.

"Don't you get it?" Ramsey asked, scooting forward on the couch to turn toward me. He had a way of talking with his hands that my old friend Lulu would love. "That's not the way this works. The Tellers know the future, which means they very likely knew that Abram was going to end up here. For all we know, they orchestrated everything to get him to be in that room waiting for you. Hell, they're probably aware of the conversation we're having right now and are counting the ways that it could play out."

"They can fuck themselves, then." I snorted. "If they're listening to this conversation, or if they already have from some future vision, I want them to know they can fuck themselves and I'll die before I let someone I love be owned." My heartrate picked up and I felt like I was starting to hyperventilate.

"Charisse—"

His voice broke through the waves that had started crashing in my head, and brought me back to earth. I took a few deep breaths before I was able to answer him.

"I won't have that, Ramsey," I said finally. "Not for one minute. I'm not fighting as hard as I am just to let some self-righteous douchebags who think they know better than everyone else treat people like they don't matter. I haven't given everything I love up for this. I would never—"

A picture fell from inside the living room and thudded hard to the floor. Glass shattered across the apartment's beige carpet.

"Damnit," I muttered. I hated not being able to control my emotions.

Sometimes, the magic inside me came rushing out at times like this, and it sucked that it happened and actually destroyed something.

I stood and crossed the room to the picture's remains. Tucked behind the broken frame was an aged paper, probably at least a decade old, and if not, certainly as yellowed as I'd expect an old piece of paper to be.

With a sigh, I knelt down and took a closer look. I lifted the page and unfolded it to reveal the neatly scrawled words, unable to control the shiver that ran down my spine as I read the words to myself.

WE'RE NOT SELF-RIGHTEOUS, and if you want to stand a chance at getting out of this alive, might I suggest going for coffee? You might find you'll get more than the caffeine out of it.
Your Friend, Darla

"IS-IS THIS FOR ME?" I asked, holding the letter out toward Ramsey with a raised eyebrow and a shaking hand.

He stood to join me, adjusted his glasses on his nose, and took his time while he read the proffered letter.

"I think it must be," he said nervously. "You did just call them self-righteous."

"Damn." I flopped on the couch and dropped my head back to stare at the ceiling. "Just when I thought things couldn't get any creepier."

I WASN'T sure what to do after that, honestly. I hadn't planned on getting a letter pre-written for me by some strange mystic and left in my apartment so that I could unveil it with my magical outburst.

Though, given just how screwed up my life had been, maybe I should have expected it. As it stood, with nothing better to go on, I was left without many options. I decided to do what the letter suggested and go out for coffee. Though, because I wasn't exactly sure of what was happening, I took Huntsman with me.

"You know," he said as we walked down the busy city sidewalk, "you don't have to bring me with you everywhere you go. I'm not going to run off."

I stared at him sideways and scrunched my nose at his asinine statement. "That thought hadn't occurred to me, but now that you mention it…"

"Your home is too small for guests," he countered, pushing open the door to the first coffee shop we crossed.

I crossed my arms against the air-conditioned chill as I scanned for an open table, not able to find one through the crowd. "I have a guest room. And a couch. I'd bet it beats living in a bottle."

Huntsman sighed heavily as he plodded over to a table by the window that I hadn't noticed during my scan of the shop. He waited for me to take a seat, then sat down across from me at the table. Dark circles shadowed his eyes, and the way he sat in the small metal chair…it was more like he'd sunk into it than actually sat down.

Gone was the strong, confident Huntsman that I'd known from the past. Even the nutty aroma of strong, freshly brewed coffee didn't seem enough to energize him, and I suspected drinking a cup wouldn't do much better. There was nothing I could do to bring him out of this funk, and I didn't even know where to start.

Magic was stronger than caffeine, and the magic placed on Huntsman was slowing him down in a way that no amount of coffee could help.

I followed his gaze to a couple sitting a few tables away from us. They were smiling, sipping at drinks, nibbling on scones like there was nothing that could destroy their day. They didn't know about the darkness of this world or the monsters lurking just around the corner. All they knew was the natural light shining through an adorable coffee shop window. They saw the light in the young man's eyes, the color of the young woman's bubblegum pink pants, and the sun glinting off the buckle of the tan purse she had slung over the corner of her chair back. They were oblivious to everything around them.

"I wish this day would never end," the woman said, beaming across the table at her man.

My heart lurched at that. In another lifetime, that was the life Abram and I could have had.

I was wondering if Huntsman was having the same thought, about himself and perhaps a woman he used to have in his life, when he rocked to his feet and approached their table.

"Can I get you anything?" he asked the couple. "Anything you wish."

I grabbed his arm and pulled him back toward our table, but he didn't budge. Did he think this was the person we were meeting?

The young woman smiled up at him, but her body coiled back in her chair. "Um, we're good. Thanks."

The guy sitting across from her stood. "Do you work here?"

I hooked my arm around Huntsman's and tried again to guide him back to the table.

"No," Huntsman said, not moving. "I was simply wondering if you wished for anything."

"Huntsman," I whispered sharply through my teeth. "*Sit. Down.*"

"Do you know him?" the girl asked, leveling her gaze at me. In that moment, I didn't feel so bad for her discomfort anymore. *Obviously* I knew him. What kind of question was that?

"*Huntsman,*" I hissed again, pulling more firmy.

He paused another beat before slowly backing away. He plopped back into his chair at our table and let out a puff of air.

"What was that about?" I growled. "You're acting strange."

Huntsman frowned and shook his head. "I don't know. I guess... I guess I thought maybe...they wanted something? I feel as though I need to do something for someone. I need to make their wishes come true."

I grimaced. Huntsman was changing before my eyes. The man who had come to mean so much to me was disappearing, only to be replaced by a weaker version of himself. A genie. A prisoner. A servant meant to grant someone's wish.

I was going to lose him, and worse than that, he was going to lose himself. We both knew it, and I wasn't sure if there was anything either of us could do. Not that he actually wanted to do anything about it.

"Are we sure this is the right place?" he asked finally, leaning forward on the table and leveling me with his glare.

"Not even a little bit," I said honestly. I lifted the menu as if I planned to pick something, but I couldn't focus on the words on the page. "The letter said to get coffee. So, here I am, getting coffee. I'd have to imagine that an oracle or a mystic or whatever the person who wrote the letter identifies as would know where I was going to end up." I shrugged. "My guess is that it would be the same way she'd know exactly where to put the letter."

"Look at you," a voice chimed from over us with laughter trickling through the air.

I jerked my head up, and the menu fell from my grasp back to the table. Standing beside us was a short woman with a pink pixie cut and a bright smile, staring down at me. In her hand was a pot of coffee, and on her shirt, a name tag that read Stacey.

"Look at how smart you are," she cooed. "You figured the whole thing out. We knew you would."

I glared at her, instantly aware that the woman I was looking at was either the person who wrote the letter or had something to do with the Tellers, the group that Ramsey had told me were responsible for the marking on Abram's body. My body tensed, and I prepared myself that something was about to happen. What, exactly, I didn't have a clue.

Glancing at her nametag, I smirked. "You're Darla, I assume?"

"No," the woman said, pointing at her name tag uselessly. "The name's Stacey, obviously. Darla was my great-great grandmother."

"Your what?" I asked, my heart skipping a beat while I tried to figure out exactly what was going on around me. "But the letter—"

"Yeah," Stacey answered and cut me off, her smile widening. "We've been waiting for you for a long time, Charisse Bellamy. Longer than you could ever imagine."

CHAPTER 15

It's weird enough when a stranger knows your name. It's weirder, though, when they know it because their great-great-grandmother had foreseen this very moment years before you had ever been born.

That's where I was currently sitting. In a cafe, with Huntsman, while I stared at a woman who knew enough about my life to freak me out.

"We should take a walk," Stacey, the weirdo who knew those things, said from where she stood next to Huntsman and me. Her eyes brightened and her smile widened impossibly more as she set the coffeepot on the cheap formica table of the coffee shop.

"You're at work," I said, trying to buy myself some time from having to be alone with this woman. "You can't leave when you're at work."

It was insane of me to say; I knew that even as she was staring at me with wide eyes. With all that was going on, the idea of Stacey working being the thing that would stop us from continuing this conversation was ridiculous. Still, my mind had to go somewhere, and that was what it decided on.

"Oh yeah," Stacey said, scrunching up her nose and

turning to the front of the coffee shop. "Hey, Carl. I quit, okay?"

Without even breaking stride, she popped off her apron, letting her name tag fall to the floor.

I was completely dumbfounded, feeling like I was stuck in an episode of the Twilight Zone. I mean, I lived with a mage, and magic was normal to me. This, however, was *not* something I was used to. No one in New York just quit their job when they wanted to take a walk. Money was hard to come by.

A balding man who looked like the world had chewed him up and spit him out stared at Stacey blankly before he shrugged. "Okay."

Then he turned back to helping customers as though one of his employees hadn't just quit in the middle of their rush. It didn't seem he expected anyone to stick around this hole in the wall for long.

I looked around, hoping that a few of the other customers felt the same way I did, and was sort of happy when I saw the astonished looks on a few other occupants' faces.

Stacey sashayed back to the table, excitement on her face as if today were Christmas. "Well, now that I've quit and that's done," she said cheekily. "Meet you outside."

She walked out, not once looking back to see if we were following her. If my eyes were even half as wide as Huntsman's, I should have been able to see clear to the moon.

"Are we actually going to follow her?" Huntsman asked, glancing from me to outside and back again.

Stacey had already pushed through the coffee shop door to stand on the sidewalk. A sea of yellow cabs whizzed on the street behind her.

I stood, clearing my throat. "We've already come this far. We might as well see the damn thing through."

Huntsman stood and followed me as I walked out of the coffee shop, his footsteps clomping behind me in lazy thuds.

Stacey was still standing on the sidewalk, her light pink pixie-cut hair appearing more silvery in the sunlight. She flicked the ash off a cigarette before taking another drag.

I folded my arms across my chest and glared at her. I honestly couldn't believe what I'd just seen. "You quit your job just like that?"

"Sounds like you care more than Carl did," she said, hugging her midsection with one arm while the hand holding her cigarette dropped away from her mouth. "You're the only reason I was working there in the first place. It's not my fault you took longer than you should have. Lord knows it wasn't for the money. This probably won't come as a surprise, but my family is, like, freaky good at the stock market." She shrugged again. "Perks of being born into oracles, I suppose."

"The Tellers?" I corrected her, arching an eyebrow as sort of a dare for the woman to contradict me. I mean, she was the one to call them oracles, and everything Ramsey had told me was that they went by a different name.

Though it wasn't much in the way of information, and it certainly was nothing compared to what she obviously knew about me, I wanted Stacey to know she wasn't the only one around here with information about what was going on.

It was all a waste though. If this little challenge affected her at all, she didn't let on.

She probably already knew that I would know this. Or say that, or whatever. If I thought about it for any amount of time, I'd lose my mind. It was just like running around in circles. Almost like asking whether or not the chicken or the egg came first.

"Yep," she chimed, grinning a little, then bit her lower lip as her gaze moved over to Huntsman. "You're kind of a dish, aren't you?" Her voice was practically flirty, and if she'd been anyone else, I might have called her on it.

"A dish?" Huntsman asked, looking from me to the woman and back again. "A dish of what?"

If we were in any other situation, it would be hilarious to see him struggling to deal with Stacey flirting with him.

"I'd say you're a dish of whatever you want, sexy," Stacey purred, her smile widening. "My favorite is whipped cream and strawberries, though." The hint in her voice was enough to make me want to gag.

I stepped between the two of them, needing to act as a buffer before my brain exploded from the sexual vibes. "Enough of that. You pulled me away from my home, away from my work. You say you and your family know everything about me? Then you should know I don't have time to waste. So, unless you want to be magically twisted into the human equivalent of a pretzel, I suggest you start explaining yourself."

Stacey blinked while she was staring directly at me, and something passed over her face, though it wasn't fear. Instead, it looked like curious bemusement. "I had a feeling you might say that."

She chuckled at her own joke, looked away, and shook her head as she took another puff of her cigarette while staring into space.

She must have known that, regardless of what she said or did next, I wasn't going to follow through on magically assaulting her. I wasn't that kind of Conduit. I wasn't that kind of woman. Still, making threats had become a habit. Usually it went a long way, but it was starting to sink in that that wouldn't be the case when it came to the Tellers.

Still, her reaction told me quite a bit about her character. Even things I'm sure she didn't really want me to know. Although, to play devil's advocate, she probably knew exactly what she was doing.

Well, I'd prove us both wrong. I *would* be that kind of Conduit today.

"You don't have to do that," Stacey said.

My hand hadn't even clasped together to summon the

magic needed to send a jolt of pain through her, the offensive maneuver I was going to throw at her to prove I meant business. Still, it seemed Stacey was prepared.

"We're going to have a conversation," she continued. "It's going to be enlightening and frustrating, and you're going to end up disliking me more than you already do. But it'll prove important and necessary all the same. So, there's no need in magically twisting my arm." The woman winked at me. "Though, I have to admit, this is going to make a hell of an addition to my maid-of-honor toast at your wedding."

My jaw tightened. I didn't know if Stacey was screwing with me or not, but whatever the truth was, I didn't have time to unpack it right now. At the moment, there was no time to waste, and we needed every second we could get.

"Then start talking," I said flatly, demanding some sort of action. "What did you do to Abram?"

Stacey chuckled loudly, making me want to punch her in the boob. "Abram was a tagged animal, a light in the dark to ensure you'd come to us." She looked down at her nails, like what she was telling me wouldn't bring rage boiling to the surface. "Well, to me, I suppose. I'm the last of my family, as it turns out. At least," she said wistfully, "I am for now."

My body tensed. "Call my boyfriend an animal one more time, and no amount of convincing will stop me from twisting more than your arm."

"He's not your boyfriend, though. Is he?" Stacey asked. She dropped her cigarette to the concrete and crushed it with her shoe. "Not anymore. Sure. The Abram you knew and loved is in there *somewhere*, awake and rattling around. You made sure of that. But he's not in the driver's seat, and the thing calling the shots *is* an animal, Charisse. If you're going to have any chance at stopping what's to come, you'd be best served to remember that."

"Chance?" Huntsman asked, glaring at her. "Why would a

woman who could see everything about the future need to rely on *chance*? Why would such a woman even believe in chance?"

"Such a woman?" Stacey asked, grinning coyly. "You're a tease, aren't you?"

"I assure you, ma'am, I'm no such thing," Huntsman said. "If I took it in my head to want you in a physical way, you would not question my desires."

Stacey cut her gaze back to me. "How do you get anything done at all with this one walking around?"

"Just answer the question," I said curtly. The entire time I was waiting for her to start speaking, I tried to figure out what she would say.

"The question is flawed," Stacey said smartly. "It implies that I know everything about the future. Not only is that untrue, it's also impossible. The future is a mosaic. It's a collage of possibilities. One thing happens, and it changes a thousand others. And that happens a hundred times an hour. I don't see all of it, because even a day looking at a big picture like that would be enough to drive anyone insane. The Tellers, my family, taught me to train myself on specific things. Some of us looked at regions. Some of us looked at events. I was raised to look at individuals."

My stomach churned. "Individuals?" I knew what she was saying, though.

"Well, one select group of individuals," she answered.

"You've been watching me," I said flatly, knowing exactly what she was hinting at. "For your entire life."

"You... Oh, and your friends," Stacey confirmed with a slight nod. "All the people who have interacted, are interacting, or will interact with you in your entire life. I grew up with you guys even though you never saw me, watching you like a television series that ran through my head. You're like the cast of *Friends* to me. Which, I guess, is why I'm fangirling a bit, which is unprofessional. It's also why I was so stoked to see that I was going to get to join you. It's a dream come true for me," Stacey went on, gushing. "It's like I'm going to be part of the team, doing my part to help all of you reach your goals. Even if it is your last mission."

I was going along with her, for most of her conversation. I was used to it, honestly. I'd been a model. Not to sound cocky or anything, but there were always people who recognized me from one of my campaigns and wanted to gab about things. It was par for the course for my life. That last part, though, it stopped me in my tracks and caused my mind to come to a screeching halt while I processed it.

"Last mission?" I asked. "What are you talking about?"

"Oh, not for all of you," she amended with a placating gesture of her hands. "Don't worry," Stacey said, smiling and bringing me out of my stupor. "The rest of you are going to continue on, doing everything you've already been doing for the past few years. It's just your last mission as the group you are now. One of you won't be there for the next one. That's all. Before this is over, one of you has to die." Stacey shrugged. "That's just the way it has to go."

CHAPTER 16

Ramsey paced around the unwelcome woman as she sat at our kitchen table. She sipped on a hot tea with lemon and acted as if she hadn't just dropped the biggest bombshell in the history of bombshells at my feet just minutes ago outside that coffee shop. It was like she didn't even care that she'd just told me that someone in my circle was going to die during this next crazy mission we were on.

"I don't see why you felt the need to bring me here," Stacey said, setting down the mug that I'd used every day for the past year. It was chipped on one side; I had dropped it last week while trying to carry too many mugs from the dishwasher to the cabinet, and I remember crying because it felt like my entire life was falling apart with that mug. "I mean, I knew you were going to do it, but I still don't see the need to bring me to this craphole."

Her fingers danced along the edge of the mug. She was excited to be here, to be a part of our circle. Just like she'd said before. She was a fan.

That's when it first occurred to me. Stacey must live a lonely life. She was always on the outside, looking in. Watching our life, and never being able to participate or interact. It was almost enough for me to feel bad for her. Almost.

"The need, ma'am," Ramsey started, interrupting my thoughts, "is that you just threatened us, and now we must determine the correct level of the threat we face from you."

He didn't move a muscle as he stared at the interloper in my apartment. Instead, he watched every flinch Stacey made, and every minute movement of her body with a critical eye.

"You're always so dramatic, Ramsey," Stacey tittered, swirling her finger around the lip of the mug, this time in a flirtatious way. "I didn't threaten you any more than the weatherman forecasting an early frost threatens the crops the weather will affect. Haven't you ever heard of not shooting the messenger? Or maybe, in this case, it would be kidnapping the messenger. Although, I came willingly, so it wasn't really kidnapping."

"Of course I've thought about not shooting the messenger. Unless they deserve it." Ramsey pulled a handkerchief from his pocket and removed his glasses from their perch on his nose to clean them. It was typical Ramsey...a move made to look like he was completely unaffected, when in reality he was on high alert just waiting for the room to explode in chaos so he could act. "I'm just not quite sure that you're the messenger, or innocent for that matter. For all I know—for all *any* of us know—you might be the gunsman. After all, you and your people did infect our friend with God knows what."

I looked at Huntsman, surprised at the sheer volume of what he'd just said. Usually, he kept it light, using barely enough words to get his point across. He really must have a problem with the girl sitting at our table.

"He hasn't been infected with anything," Stacey said, rolling her eyes at Ramsey. Her thumb rubbed down the hand of the mug, still flirting with Huntsman and unashamed to be doing it in front of us. "Again, you're being dramatic. Like I told Charisse and that extra-special hunk of man meat over there, what was put on Abram was a tag, a brand. It was something that was meant to ensure this moment happened, that I could and would be found by you when I needed it to happen. That I would be brought here. To you."

She batted her eyes, and I fought the urge to gag.

At this, Huntsman leaned forward on the kitchen counter, gripping the ledge so hard I thought the formica might split under his grip. Stacey stared at his hands with wide eyes, and I could see the way her mind was turning with his movements. There was something there, besides the obvious attraction she had to him. Huntsman didn't say anything, but I knew that if this woman did anything to make him cross, he'd make her regret it without even breaking a sweat. He'd probably enjoy it, too.

I wonder if she knew as much, given she seemed to know everything.

While I watched her face, I realized that she did. I knew the look on her face. I'd worn it myself with Abram multiple times. Excitement and trepidation all rolled into one.

I took my opening. It was an opportunity to hold my own with the woman while Huntsman continued to act with controlled restraint. If I wasn't sure that she knew what was coming, I might approach it with unbridled glee, but there was a growing part of me that thought she was ready for what was coming next.

"Why, exactly, did you want to be brought here?" I asked, arching my eyebrows at the woman. "You just said you didn't see why I felt the need to bring you, and yet you've been planning on it for who knows how long."

"Because that's what happens in the version of events that we need to happen." She set down the mug, and I realized that I hadn't even seen her pick it up again. "In every version of the future where you have a chance of winning the storm that's coming our way, I come here. In the futures where I don't come here, you guys don't fare so well, and more than one of you get killed. Which means the world doesn't fare so well, either. Like Armageddon level destruction heads our way. So, while I don't know what possessed you to do so, you bringing me here is kind of important."

Stacey waved her hand in the air, giving off a sense of nonchalance that none of the rest of us were feeling.

"So, what you're saying," I said before pausing. Really, I was afraid to say what I was thinking. It was ridiculous, but I knew it was the truth. "Is that you being here is the special sauce that makes us surviving this possible?" I blinked hard, remembering what she'd said earlier. "Well, some of us anyway."

I took a deep breath and fought past the knot that had risen up in my throat. It hurt, knowing that one of us was going to die.

"You're the one who said it. Not me," she said. "And I don't know if that's exactly right, either. Maybe me being here just sets something else in motion that needs to happen. I don't write the future, you know."

After replacing his glasses on his face, Ramsey stepped in front of her, arms crossed, facing me where I stood on the other side of the table. "First of all, she's lying to us," he said defiantly. He turned his body slightly to stick one of his arms to indicate Stacey, then crossed his arms again and leaned against the counter. "Probably about everything, but certainly about the eye stamp on Abram's body. It's brimming with magic, and you wouldn't get that from a tag simply meant to ensure something happens."

A snort from our guest drew my attention away from him. "As far as *you* know, you wouldn't get that from a tag," Stacey said. The feet of her chair screeched against the table as she stood. "I have magic you've never seen before. Magic you wouldn't and couldn't even begin to understand."

"*Securitos*," I said, simply. The word, pulling at power from deep inside of me, pulled Stacey back into her chair, securing her and planting her hands flat against the table.

Normally, I didn't need to actually say the word to cast the spell. I just didn't want to test anything or give her the chance to escape. I didn't know how the power of a Teller worked, and I wasn't about to test it out. Not when we needed her to answer us.

"That wasn't necessary, either," Stacey said, looking up at me. But instead of looking angry or offended, her expression remained unaffected. "I'm not a danger to anyone here. I told you, I grew up with you guys. I don't want to see you hurt."

"Stop saying that," I commanded with a bite to my tone that I hadn't meant to be there. "It's weird. Besides, if you want to prove you're not a danger to any of us, it would be helpful if you started by telling us the truth. The whole truth. What are you really doing here? And what do you want?"

"I'm here to help you get through this," she answered simply. She took her time as we stared at her collectively. "I'm here to help you stop The Brothers."

She'd literally just said the one thing that would cause me to pause. The one thing that might get Ramsey off her case for the moment, and that might cause Huntsman to give her a little bit of breathing room from his threats.

I tapped Ramsey's shoulder, and he stepped aside. I appreciated that he was trying to provide some kind of barrier of protection between Stacey and me, but I could handle myself. Or I should be able to, anyway.

"The Brothers?" I asked tentatively.

My heart jumped a little at the thought of it. After all this time, I still didn't know much about them. Other than the fact that they seemed to be all-powerful beings who wanted me dead, the duo was basically a big question mark for me.

But, as it turned out, that might not be true for Stacey.

I ran my manicured fingernails across my bottom lip as I considered the implications. If she were telling the truth about things—and that was a *big* if—then she might know something about The Brothers. She might know a way to take them out. She might even know how all of this ends.

But, if she did, was there really any way I could trust her?

"You can," she said, glaring at me. "You can trust me."

It was as though she could read my mind, as though she knew exactly what my thoughts had been. Maybe she had. Maybe she knew everything that was going to happen, and she was just playing us all like reruns of America's Next Top Model.

"I've been watching you guys my entire life," she repeated, "and maybe that *is* weird—"

"It is," I confirmed with a nod and a slightly barbaric grinding of my teeth.

"but it also means I consider you my friends. Soon enough, if things go the way they're supposed to, I'll consider you my family, and you'll do the same for me." She was convinced that what she was saying was the truth, clearly.

Stacey shook her head. It was the only part of her body that could move right now under my spell. Considering that, maybe she really couldn't predict everything that would happen.

"I know we're not there yet...the you trusting me part," she went on. "But we're in a precarious position, one that you don't understand. We're standing on the edge of something horrible, and if we don't save Huntsman, it means we won't save the world."

Huntsman stepped around the counter and toward the woman. "Explain yourself," he demanded, all that controlled reserve gone now from his posture. "What are you talking about?"

"I know you're big on the 'self-sacrifice' train, Huntsy," Stacey said, eliciting a grimace from Huntsman. "I know you'd give yourself freely and allow yourself to suffer for the rest of eternity stuck in a lamp before you let anything happen to anyone in this room, but that's not a possibility, I'm afraid. At the end of this, you'll be needed just like the rest of us. The Brothers can't be defeated and the world can't be saved if you're not here to help save it, to help do what must be done. I've seen too many variants of the upcoming war and the lives that can be lost. I told you. The only ones where we stand a chance have you in that room with Abram today. They have you here in this room. They have *you*. You're one of the only constants in a storm full of variables. Because of that, you can't give up. You can't let the hunger growing in your soul win and deprive you of your uniqueness."

Huntsman scoffed with what I knew was false bravado. "Shows what you know. I would never give up."

"But you would," I said quietly, realizing just what was at stake here. "For me, for the people you care about, you'd give up your life. You know she's right."

"There's nothing dishonorable about giving your life for the right cause," Huntsman answered quickly, as though it were something he had been training to say for decades.

"Of course there isn't," I said. I sat in the chair across from Stacey and sank my head into my hands, the baby pink tips of my painted fingernails pushing into my hairline. "But, when the world is at stake, there's really only one cause that matters. I can't allow you to give up your life if your life is what saves humanity. It just wouldn't be right, regardless of how noble it might feel at the time."

"You're still assuming she's telling the truth," Ramsey said, stepping forward again and staring at Stacey with unyielding and unforgiving eyes. "We have no idea what's really going on in her head."

"But you will," Stacey said. "You'll cast the spell that'll let Charisse see into my thoughts, into my intentions, and then she'll believe me, which means all of you will believe me." She shook her head. "I just wish you could do it now."

She bit her thumb and stared at the watch on her wrist.

The one I hadn't seen before that moment. She was waiting for something, and I couldn't figure out what. I'd given up trying to predict what was happening with her. She had proven time and time again in the past few hours of our acquaintance that she knew more than I did.

"That's not a bad idea," Ramsey said, moving another step closer to Stacey. "And why wouldn't we be able to do it now?"

"Because of the scream," she said simply.

"The scream?" I asked. "What—"

Before the words could leave my mouth, Abram's screams permeated the room and surrounded us all as though he were right there. My heart leapt, wondering just what was happening in the room beyond my line of sight.

My gaze moved over to Stacey, who was looking at the door of the room where Abram was being held. Her eyes were wide and full of the knowledge of what had caused him that much pain.

"He's not alone."

CHAPTER 17

My ENTIRE BODY clenched as another pained howl escaped Abram's lips from the room where he was effectively trapped.

Yes, I knew he wasn't the man I loved, but the man I loved was still in there somewhere. Whatever was happening to him, whatever was hurting those arms and legs and heart, was doing it to the same arms and legs and heart that had come to mean the entire world to me.

I couldn't allow that.

A surge of power rushed through me, and I soon saw that I wasn't standing at all. I was floating. I was hovering above the floor, power emanating from me in what felt like tidal waves.

"What is this?" I asked.

"I don't know," Stacey answered. "You never tell me."

"What do you—"

"We can't get in," she said. "Only you're able to. And in every timeline, for all the time we know each other afterward, you never tell me what was in that room." She shook her head, her pink pixie cut hair trembling with the movement. "You only ever say that it changed everything, and that I should have told you to go in there sooner. I've listened to you cry, drunkenly, as you beg me to do it faster the next time. I've heard you rage about your hatred of me for not doing it. I'm not going to put up with it in this timeline, too." She pointed her hand toward the door. "So go, damn it! Before you hate me all over again."

Another rush of energy moved through me, and a torrent of magic flushed through my body as I found myself flying toward the door against my will. My hands balled into fists as I neared it, ready to slam into the thing as opposed to actually turning the knob.

I couldn't control this magic; it wasn't mine. Stacey had been right. She did have power that I couldn't understand. The fact that she was able to do this to me was astounding. Especially with all the protection spells we had cast. All of those thoughts flew through my mind while I careened toward the door.

As it turned out, trying to turn the knob would be a mistake.

The moment I slammed into the door, something hit me...something *other* than the door.

I flinched, expecting it to be hard or powerful, or even something that might tear me apart. During all the things I'd been through in the last few years, ever since I found out the truth about who I was and what I was capable of, my life and even my body had been hit with things constantly trying to hurt and destroy me. There were demons and beasts and more than a few jolts of magically offensive forces that attempted to take me off my feet, throw me off-balance, or just downright kill me without any sort of hesitation.

No one would be surprised to learn I was expecting that, given all I had been through. Yet, what hit me was something else entirely.

Something *good*. Something *right*.

As I moved through the door, passing harmlessly through the solid object without so much as breaking stride or getting a splinter, peace flowed through me the likes of which I had never felt before.

It was like coming home. No. It was better than that. It was like finally realizing where home was after a lifetime of searching. It was like the last page of a book where all your favorite characters get everything they ever wanted and none of the antagonists survive. It was finally finding rest after a lifetime of torment that was meant to destroy your soul.

After passing through that door, my body shuddered from the sensation, and I was forced to blink repeatedly to see the room and its occupants.

There, on the tan carpeted floor, his legs bent under him, sat Abram. His eyes were trained at something on the ceiling, something I couldn't see myself but was there without a doubt.

He didn't appear to be in any pain. He wasn't afraid or upset. Instead, he, too, looked at peace. As though he were living in a moment he wished could stretch out into forever.

"Charisse," he said, and his voice held all the love and familiarity it had carried when he was mine.

I knew, in that instant, I wasn't in the presence of the thing that took over the man I loved. It was gone, even if only for a few moments. Abram was here. He was back, and I was going to make the most of it. I didn't have a choice. It was like the missing piece of my soul was staring up at me.

"She says you can't see it, Charisse," he continued while staring at the ceiling. "She says no one can see it yet. But you will."

I rushed toward him, not caring about what he was saying right then. We had time for all of that later. I collapsed onto my knees and wrapped my arms around him, never wanting this moment to end. Tears burned at the back of my eyelids as I closed them tightly against the oncoming emotions.

While I pressed my head into the crook of his shoulder, another wave of peace ran through me. This moment in time was even better than any I could possibly have imagined. Just the feeling of being in his arms again, of wrapping myself around the love of my life, was enough to give me ecstasy.

"It's all the same hand," Abram said. "I can see it all now. It's always been the same hand, ever since the very beginning. It's all so obvious. It always had to be this way." He was rambling, his voice almost incoherent and strained. But I made out every word and stored it away for later.

"Baby, I don't know what you mean," I admitted, kissing his neck and hoping the things he was saying weren't because of some brain damage brought on by all that had happened to him. "I need you to come with me. I need you to let Ramsey see you. Maybe, if he can actually take a look at what happens to you when you come back to yourself, he can make it permanent." I was being irrational, but I needed to do something. I had to hope that there was some way to undo the damage.

"This isn't about that, Charisse," Abram said. "This isn't about any of that. You can't tell them this. You can't tell anyone about what's happening. They're not meant to understand."

"What do you mean?" I pulled away from him, furrowing my eyebrows while trying to wrap my mind around what he was saying. "What are you talking about?"

Before he could answer, his body seized up, and he passed out.

"Abram!" I said, shaking him. His tanned olive skin turned sallow, almost pale with his dark hair matted against his time-worn skin. "Abram, come back to me!"

"You're still not asking the right questions. How many times did I tell you to ask the right questions and not to let your emotions get the better of you?" An achingly and annoyingly familiar voice chimed from behind me.

Turning, I saw none other than Satina standing there, a bright glow surrounding her. She was dressed strangely, at least for the fact that she was standing in my apartment. It was as though she had stepped out the titanic, right out of the ballroom and transplanted into the room with me.

"Didn't I teach you anything?" she asked, the same wry smirk on her lips as always.

My heart might as well have skidded to a stop. Of all the things I thought I might come into contact with in this room, Satina was definitely not one of them. Especially since she'd been dead for over a year.

Though, I had to admit, there's no way that I should be surprised. The feeling I experienced when coming into the room—that peace, that safety—I hadn't felt since the moment Satina took her last breath on this world and gave me freedom from her machinations. The idea that it came back with her just seemed perfect enough. Of course, that didn't mean I wasn't allowed to have questions.

I wanted to stand, but Abram was still here, still cradled in my arms and just as heavy as he'd always been. Bouncing between the two of them would be like being torn into equal pieces and being expected to survive it. Both of them were people I loved. Both of them were people I was sure I'd never see again. Now that they were both back, albeit in strange and unpredictable manners, I wasn't sure how to react. I wasn't sure how to respond.

My mouth went dry, and my body shook with something like fear or anticipation.

"Is that really you?" I asked cautiously.

"Still not the right question," Satina said. As always, she had that air of amusement about her, as if, despite my dire situation and her desire for me to fix it, she still found it all entertaining. "You know it's me, Charisse. You can see it. More than that, you can feel it. I only have a short time here. Don't waste it by confirming that which you already know to be true or by questioning me about things that don't matter."

Her voice was a scolding thing, as though I had been

called into the principal's office and this was what was awaiting me there. Still, I knew her well enough to know there was love in it. Satina wouldn't do anything unless it was in my best interest, even if sometimes it didn't feel that way.

Steadying myself, I searched my mind for the right questions, for the things I honestly had no clue about. Wherever Satina came from, wherever she was watching us from, it was clear she had more information about the trouble I was in than I did. I couldn't waste even a second of that.

"Can I win this?" I asked, then swallowed hard as I decided to go for broke. "The Brothers—can I beat them?"

"Define win," she said quickly. "Or beat, for that matter." She shook her ethereal head. "The Brothers are Eternals, Charisse. Nothing we do or don't do can change that. If killing them is your goal, then I'm afraid you're climbing an insurmountable hill and you're only going to fail and kill everyone around you while you do it. But that doesn't mean there aren't other choices. It doesn't mean the things that hunt you won't also be the things that save you. The things that go bump in the night might just be your greatest allies when all of this is said and done."

"What's that supposed to mean?" I asked. "How am I supposed to figure that out?" Why did everything she said always have to be some kind of riddle meant to annoy the hell out of me?

"Wrong question," Satina answered with a mischievous smile. "And please hurry. You have no idea how difficult being here is for me. The only reason I was even able to do it was because of her help."

"*Her?*" I asked.

"Someone who loves you very much," Satina said. She didn't smirk when she said it, though. Instead, her strained grin turned to a grimace. If I didn't know Satina better, I might even think that glint in her eyes was sorrow instead of mischievousness. "Now, please, ask what you need, not what you want. I'm afraid, even with her help, I can't hold this connection much longer. Unfortunately, I'm bound from telling you the answer unless you ask the question directly."

I wanted to ask a lot of things. I wanted to find out who Satina was talking about when she said someone 'loved me very much.' I wanted to ask her where she had been. I wanted to find out about life after death. I wanted to know everything, but that wasn't what I needed.

I had work to do. I couldn't afford to indulge myself, to tend to the questions of my own mind or heart, when the world was at stake.

"How do I do it?" I asked mournfully. "How do I save the world?"

A smile graced the Conduit's beautiful face, the likes of which I'd never seen before. It transformed her from a monster in my eyes, to a beautiful young woman once more.

"That's the right question," she said. "You have to make the right choice. The time will come, and it will come soon, where this entire chaotic war will dance on the head of a needle. To make it right, you have to follow your head and heart as one." She looked at the doorway. "I'm with you Charisse, even when you can't see me. Someone out there beyond the door isn't. There's a traitor to you here, Charisse. A foe disguised as a friend. There's someone who doesn't want you to succeed, who will stop at nothing to see you fail and destroyed at the hands of The Brothers. Find them, fix it all, and above all, make the right choice. I know you can do it. It's what you were destined to do."

With that, as I blinked back tears and tried not to sob at the genuine emotion she was showing me, Satina faded away. I was left in an almost empty room with only my thoughts and fears as company.

~

My head was still spinning and my heart was racing with everything that had happened in that room. Seeing Satina was a trip, but the thing that stuck out in my mind the most, the thing that threatened to rip me apart, was what she'd told me about my friends.

She said there was a traitor among the people standing outside that room. At least I knew Abram wasn't here to kill me. Well, not while he was asleep at least.

Now, deductive reasoning would tell me the traitor had to be Stacey. I'd just met the woman. I didn't know her from Adam, and she purported to know everything there was to know about me. She was the easy choice.

The thing was, she might have been too easy. I had been at this long enough to know things weren't always as they seemed. What was more, Stacey wasn't wrong. She obviously had some sort of foreknowledge at her disposal. She hadn't lied to me yet. At least, not in a way I could prove.

But if it wasn't her… I shook my head, not ready to let myself have the thought just yet. Well, the thought was there that if it was her, she'd know that I knew. Especially if she knew all of the different futures. Maybe it *was* her. It could still possibly be her. It could be someone who wouldn't destroy me to know they had betrayed my friendship.

But then, Stsacey wasn't my friend yet. Did what Satina say apply to future friends? But then, I wouldn't be her friend in the future if she betrayed me. I wanted to believe she was the traitor, but it just didn't line up.

I wasn't sure how I was going to proceed with the information that I'd gotten, but whatever way it was, I had to be careful around all of them, which left me with a bitter taste in my mouth. Ramsey had been my confidant for a year, and Huntsman had proven over and over again that he could be trusted. For the upteenth time in a day, I wanted to scream in frustration.

"I don't understand why you can't just tell us what

happened in there," Ramsey whined as he paced around the kitchen and stared at me as though I was crazy.

"Because I can't." I rolled my eyes. "So, can we just drop it?" I asked, tension obvious in my fraying voice. "We have bigger problems to worry about anyway." I looked over at Huntsman, another of my friends, another possible traitor. "Like making sure he's not turned into a genie."

"Djinn," Ramsey corrected me.

"Like I could give a damn," I snapped. "You said there was a way to find the genie using Abram."

"There is," Ramsey explained. "I did some research while you were in there...doing whatever it was you were doing for hours on end that you won't tell us about." He coughed and then went on as though he hadn't just acted like a petulant child who didn't get his way. "I found a spell that will work, but I'm not sure you're going to like it."

I'd heard that before. Repeatedly. From him. Regarding this whole thing.

"Honestly, I'm not sure I care at this point," I answered honestly. "What do I have to do?"

Ramsey scoffed. "Don't worry. I'm not going to ask you to do anything you haven't done before."

CHAPTER 18

"This is ridiculous," I said, staring at Abram through the open doorway and shaking my head. "There has to be another way. I can't do this. I...I just won't."

Ramsey, standing next to me with arms crossed over his chest, sighed as he answered. "I'm sorry, Char, but there is no other way. The spell was clear. You have to be joined with Abram for it to work, and since things went horribly wrong the last time we tried to mentally join the two of you, physical joining is all we have on the table right now."

"That's easy for you to say," I answered, glaring at the man who used to be the love of my life and feeling my heart break all over again. "You're asking me to be close to him. You're asking me to betray what I have with Abram for this thing that's infiltrated his body."

"That's not what this is," Ramsey said, shaking his head. "No one is asking you to have sex with him for the spell to work." He turned away while a blush crept up his cheeks. "Although, I've run across more than a few incantations that are fueled by erotic energy. This isn't about that. This is about literal, physical closeness." Ramsey held his hands together, indicating what he was talking about. "And of course it isn't easy for me. You're my friend, Char. These days, you're my best, and pretty much only, friend. If you think the idea of putting you in an uncomfortable situation is at all a simple decision for me to make, then you obviously don't know me very well." In a jerk of movement, Ramsey slammed his hands on the table and hung his head in defeat. "I don't know any other way for this to work."

A rush of guilt ran through me when I saw how tortured he was, putting me in this position. In my heart, I knew Ramsey was just trying to do this for the benefit of all of us. Finding the genie and figuring this out meant finding a way to save Huntsman. Saving Huntsman apparently also might mean finding a way to save the world, and that was more important than my momentarily discomfort.

I hung my head in my hands, unsure of what to say or do. Things had gotten so complicated. So *hard*. I had already given so much of myself in the last few months. Part of my soul that I would never be able to get back. The idea that I was going to have to give more—that even after doing it, all of this might still fail spectacularly—weighed on my mind.

That wasn't the only thing weighing on my mind, though. Satina's words were playing on repeat in my brain, digging into me like the pointed edge of a rusty fork. She told me there was a traitor in the group, among my most trusted allies and friends.

The very notion was setting my teeth on edge and giving me a migraine the size of which I'd never experienced before. It was making me doubt—not only the people around me, but myself and my abilities as well. Doubt, that I knew for an absolute fact, would be all of our downfall.

A traiter that had wormed their way into my inner circle, with the people I was closest to, that meant I was blind. I allowed it to happen. I let them in.

What kind of idiot would do that? What kind of person would let her guard down that much?

I let the doubt eat away at me, because *I* was that stupid. I let someone into my circle, and they were standing in front of me, no doubt thinking they had the upper hand. And I had no way of knowing who it was. Obviously, I wasn't capable of saving the world. That was about the only thing that I was sure of.

"Can we just stop for a minute?" I asked, forcing myself to take a deep breath, turning on my heels, and heading back to the living room before I broke down completely. Ramsey's footsteps followed. "You know I didn't mean that I don't trust you or that I don't know you," I said, plopping myself on the couch. "But this is a lot. You expect me to go in there, strip naked, watch him strip naked, and then hold hands as we tell each other our feelings. You have to understand how hard that's going to be for me. How easy it's going to be for me to slip back into thinking that the man with me belongs to me."

I started to get choked up, so I stopped talking. Instead, I focused on my fingers, twining them together and trying not to show how frustrated and nervous I was about the whole situation.

"Of course I understand that," Ramsey said. He sat down, the weight of what he was asking driving him down into the couch as though he was carrying a boulder. "But I'm not the one asking for you to do it. This is about what's necessary for the magic to take effect, Char. The fact that you can even do it is a miracle."

"Doesn't feel very miraculous," I muttered petulantly and tapped my fingers impatiently on the table.

When he stared at me with the same look in his eyes that he'd used every time I pushed back when he was trying to teach me something, I decided maybe it was time for me to shut up and listen to him. At least for a few minutes.

"Well, it is," Ramsey shot back, after what felt like forever. "The specifics of this spell are insane, to say the least. It can't be spread over more than two people at one time, and it needs both Supplicant and Conduit energy signatures to work."

Ramsey ticked everything he said off on his fingers, like he was making a list, and continues. "As well as a deep, profound connection with the host you're trying to exploit while using the spell."

He took a deep breath, and shook his head at the look on my face. There was no mistaking the fact that I was in shock, especially with all of the very specific items he was identifying.

"Make no mistake," he went on, "all of this means that you are, very likely, the only being *in the world* who can perform this spell, and that Abram is the only being in the world you can perform it on."

What Ramsey was saying didn't make any sense, and I told him so. "Why would someone create a spell only one person can use? That only *I* could use, and only on Abram, for that matter? He's been gone for a year. How would they know we'd cross paths again?"

"Maybe they saw you coming," Stacey interjected as she walked into the room, digging a spoon into a giant bowl of vanilla ice cream and smiling widely. "Maybe they created the spell because they knew you'd need it one day, but they wanted to keep that sort of power away from those who might use it to do harm or destroy the world. Maybe they forged it with a specific set of hoops that they knew only you could jump through." She licked the spoon, smiling even wider and looking like an absolute maniac. "Of course, that's just a guess."

I groaned, realizing what was going on here. "You're not serious," I said, indignation flooding me as I leapt to my feet. "This is your people? The Wandering Watchers or whatever?"

"That's not even close to our name." Stacey set the bowl on the counter next to the sink with a soft thud. "Although I suppose that you already know that, and that it's not important. The fact is, you have what you need, and you can do this."

"What I *need*," I said, "is a way to get this spell to work without having to deal with the thing that took over Abram's body." Although, if Stacey really were all-knowing, she would already know that.

"That's what you *want*," Stacey corrected. "And, as your future best friend and godmother to any possible children that you may or may not be having, I want you to have what you want, but I'm also here to inform you that the things you want and the things you need aren't always the same. They're just not, regardless of how much we might want them to be."

"Are you saying that I need to go in there and do this with Abram?" I didn't even bother touching her comment about her being my best friend. Or the one about any future children. "Are you saying I'm going to get something out of it? That it's more than just about saving the world."

Stacey shrugged. "I'm saying my people don't do anything for no reason. If they're the ones who created this spell, they did it knowing that it was going to get you naked in the room with the man you love, ready and willing to open your heart. That means that there's a damn good explanation for their actions, and you shouldn't spit in the way of that." She plugged her hands on her hips and glare at me. "And you can sure as hell bet it has nothing to do with some twisted idea of cruel embarrassment."

With that, I thought she was done talking. She leaned forward on the counter again, and picked up the remainder of her ice cream, before turning a cheeky smile on me. "Come on, it's not the end of the world," Stacey said before brandishing her spoon almost like a weapon and pointing it at me. "Your guy is hot, and if the stories you're going to tell me in the future are to be believed, he's insanely good in bed. There are definitely worse things in the world than being emotionally, physically, and sexually gratified." She grabbed my arm and squeezed. "I guess what I'm saying is that you should have fun while you have the chance. Even if it's not what you're expecting, or what you think you want."

Before I thought better of myself, I let the magic flow from my mind, and her hand was yanked from my arm.

I marched past her and Ramsey, ignoring the chuckle that came from her and the surprised grunt that came from him. I walked into the room and closed the door behind me before I could overthink it like I wanted to.

Abram, having already been told what was supposed to happen here, was shirtless and fiddling with the button on his jeans.

"Wait," I said, twisting the knob on the handle to lock it and holding my hand out in front of me to stop him in his tracks.

The man looked up at me, a devilish grin spreading across his face. "You'd rather if I went slow?" he practically purred at me.

He was enjoying this. More than that, he was enjoying the idea that I might be enjoying it. That's why he was going along with it without a fuss. Worse than that, he was doing it with a smile on his face and an obvious bulge in his pants.

If I was being honest, the truth was that somewhere in the darkest part of my brain, I knew that he was right. Who could blame me? The man standing in front of me was the love of my life. At least, physically he was. As much as I'd missed Abram's mind, I missed the physical contact of our bodies, too. The idea of having it back, even for a tiny little moment in time, was enough to send a shiver of unwanted anticipation down my spine.

Still, I had to make sure this man knew what was going on, and that he had as much of the truth as I could give him. I owed the Abram trapped inside his head that much. If he knew what was happening, he had to know that I was only doing this to get him back.

"I want to make one thing clear," I said, walking toward him as I began to strip off my clothes. "This is about necessity only. Nothing else. This is what has to happen in order for us to save Huntsman, in order for us to save the world. If I could do it any other way, and I do mean *any* other way, that's how I would be doing it." I dropped my shirt to the floor. "As it stands, I can't. But don't get it twisted. This—" I motioned between the two of us in an attempt to get his eyes off my chest. "—isn't something I want to do, and it's not something that we will ever be repeating."

"Whatever you say, sweetheart," Abram chuckled before he pulled his jeans down and freeing himself from the last of his clothing.

His body was as perfect and amazing as I remembered it, minus the scars and the brand. The golden glow of his deep tanned skin, the dark curls of hair on his chest, even his chiseled abs were just like I remembered. Damnit if he wasn't like a male model, minus the creepy body shaving they did. God, he had me close to moaning, just by stripping down.

I watched his body, unashamed at the desire that coursed through my veins. If I had to be this close to a man I wasn't in love with, at least it was a good view. This Abram liked to be watched, if the way his body shifted was any indication. That and the cocky smile that graced his lips while his eyes roved over my body.

Taking a deep breath, I walked over to him, not even caring that I wasn't wearing a shirt. His breath caught as I stepped up to his chest and placed my hand over his heart. The moment that our skin touched, I felt the familiar jolt of electricity that came with our contact. It was so intense that I almost went to my knees.

A year. I'd gone a year without his touch, and an entire year's worth of desire that coursed through me all at once.

Abram's hands wound their way around my almost naked abdomen. One hand wrapped around my waist, and the other crept up until he was cupping my neck. His fingers were rough, abrading as they grazed over the sensitive skin on my body. He didn't touch my breasts, or try and remove my pants. No, Abram took his time and seduced me with his touch in a way I wasn't prepared for.

It was a touch I thought I'd never have again. Abram, the only man who knew that my skin needed that tenderness. That caress without the rush. It didn't matter that Abram wasn't here, that the man touching me didn't know my body. The muscle memory was still there—it was the only explanation. His hands grasped me and held on, giving me what I needed from him.

I needed more. More than I had right now. Instinctively, I leaned forward, reaching for his lips with my own. But as much as I wanted it, I couldn't do this. I took his wrists in my hands and held them between us, breaking the contact between our bodies except for the barest of touches.

"Say it," I said with a ragged breath that I wasn't able to control. My chest heaved, and I forced the words out. "Tell me what your deepest, darkest truth is."

That's what this spell was meant for. It had to work this way. I had to have it, and I needed to get it over with as quickly as possible. As soon as it was done, I wouldn't have the opportunity to give in, to touch him again. Unfortunately for me, Abram wasn't playing along.

"No," he said gruffly and reached for me again. "You go first. I don't even know what my truth is, let alone how to express it." When my body was pressed up against his, he growled. Literally growled. His hard cock pressed into my stomach, and I couldn't help it. I leaned into him, craving the way it felt.

"You're useless," I muttered against his chest. Taking a deep breath, I searched myself until I found the thing that hurt the most. The truth that destroyed me every single time I thought about it. The truth I couldn't face even on the

149

brightest day. I closed my eyes, because I couldn't bare to look in his eyes and not see the emotions that Abram was supposed to have when he looked at me. I muttered, "I'd give up everything in this world, let it burn down to the ground, if I could have Abram back. The *real* Abram."

Abram's heart started to race; I could feel it pounding even though my eyes were closed.

"Wow," he said quietly.

"It's your turn" I said, still not looking at him. "Tell the truth that you don't want anyone to know."

"The truth is," he said before stopping suddenly.

I listened to his heart beating, not able to concentrate on anything but the steady rhythm as it lulled me into a false sense of comfort. I was afraid, too. Horrified to hear whatever truth he was about to spout.

"The real truth, the truth I don't want to tell anyone, and that I'll deny the second this is over…is that I wish I was that man. The one you want back in your life." He coughed, and I felt his arousal start to fade. "I wish I could be that man for you. I wish I could give him back to you."

I don't know what I expected to happen next, but the soft kiss that he pressed to my forehead wasn't it. That touch, though…it did something. As soon as his lips touched my skin, I felt a flash of clarity that I couldn't deny.

I jerked back, out of his touch and gasped as it hit me. Once I felt like I could breathe again, I finally looked up at Abram, who had somehow put his pants back on without me noticing.

"I know," I said breathlessly as I saw the same look on his face. "I know where the genie is."

CHAPTER 19

"This can't be right," Huntsman said as we stepped into the suddenly appearing rural area. He crossed his arms over his chest and peered off into the distance.

I wasn't expecting this. I most definitely wasn't prepared for it. Of all the places I expected to find the genie when the spell was cast, I never in a million years imagined it would be here. I never thought I'd come back to where life with magic had really started. To the place that almost killed me more times than I cared to admit. It was the same place, though, that had brought me to the greatest love of my life.

Huntsman looked at the rickety old bridge that held so many of my memories. "Where exactly is this place?"

"New Haven," I said, then swallowed hard as I remembered just how much this place meant to me. It was the place I met Abram for the first time. It was where Lulu and I spent the best days of our lives. It was where I last saw my father and where my mother was buried. My whole life was here, and now it seemed this genie was too. I took another deep breath, blinking back hot tears and trying to keep myself together. "This is home."

"This is where you're from?" Abram asked, looking over

at me with narrowed eyes and a look on his face that made it seem like he'd bit into a lemon. "*This* is where you grew up?"

"It's where you're from, too, in a way," I answered.

Remembering that Abram had spent many of his years in this place before we met, before I was even born, rocked me to my core. I shook my head, sighing. That didn't matter. Abram wasn't here, and explaining all of this to the man standing in his place was a mountain I didn't feel like climbing at this particular moment.

"It's a long story," was all I said to the question on his face.

"We need to get off the road and out of sight," Ramsey said, striding over to stand beside me and running a hand through his hair the way he always did when he was stressed. "This is your home, which means you'll be recognized." His gaze darted from me to Abram and back again. "Both of you. Seeing you here will only lead to questions we can't answer and serve to split our focus at a time when we certainly don't need that happening."

"There's a bomb shelter on the far side of town," Stacey said, matter-of-factly from where she stood on the other side of Huntsman.

I tried to ignore that she had a bag of chips and was crunching away on them, but I couldn't. Not when my stomach started to grumble.

She laughed and held it out, so I stuck my hand in the bag and grabbed as many chips as I could hold. I grunted in appreciation while I proceeded to stuff my face. That didn't stop me from enjoying the way the salt from the chips tasted, though. When Ramsey tried to take one of them, I slapped his hand away.

"It was built during that whole 'Russian bomb fever' thing last century," Stacey continued. "Anyway, it's filled with dried food and bottled water. There's a code, but you find it carved into the side of the building and then you tell me about it. So,

I already know." She shrugged. "If we go there, we won't be disturbed."

Stacey was really starting to piss me off. She had these interesting little tidbits like that, sometimes helpful. Sure, she was more useful than she was annoying. But I still had to wonder: if she knew these things, why did we bother going through all of this crap? If she knew we were going to end up here, why not just tell us that in the first place? Why would she make me go through the process of casting the spell, of being in that room with Abram? If she knew this was the direction we needed to go, then why not just give us everything we needed from the start and save us all the trouble?

It was infuriating.

I mean, we were standing in the middle of nowhere in freaking New Haven of all places. There was nothing in this craphole suburb that was worth coming back here for. Except for maybe Lulu.

"No," Stacey said, glaring over at me with a raised eyebrow and the hand that wasn't holding the chip bag on her hip in mock outrage.

"No, what?" I asked, batting my eyelashes at her and trying not to vocalize how pissed I really was.

"No. I couldn't have just told you we were coming here," she answered. "I get pieces. I saw you telling me the code, but not where we would need it, or when. I have a lot of the pieces, but I don't have the complete picture. And things can change. Things can happen that render some of my previous visions irrelevant."

"I didn't ask," I said, almost stupidly at this point.

It was fruitless. She knew what I was thinking, or would think, or whatever I'd apparently told her in the future, which she already knew. God, why was it such a headache to have her in my life.

"Not aloud," she replied. "But you would have if I didn't stop you, and the important thing for you to know right now is that I'm not always going to make sense. I don't know everything, and if I shared everything I knew, most of it would be wrong because there's so many versions of how this plays out."

"I'd be thrilled if I could make heads or tails of you even once when you say something. You're like if a fortune cookie's reason for being was to make sure I was late for all my appointments, and I always had a migraine, and on top of all of the rest of it, I was wearing suspenders with a dress."

I was rambling. I knew it. We all knew it. I was procrastinating, and she was letting me.

"Very funny," Stacey said. "But there are decisions you need to come to and wheels that need to begin turning based on those decisions. What comes next is completely dependent on everything happening the way it was supposed to, and even if I knew what was supposed to happen, if I told you, it might ruin it. Then the things that are meant to happen might not."

"You're making my head hurt," I admitted, rubbing soothing circles into my temples to try and get rid of the impending migraine.

"That's not me. That's the pollen," Stacey said. "And it'll go away as soon as she gives you some of your old allergy meds."

"What?" I asked. "Who are you talking about? Who is she?"

"You'll see," Stacey said with a grin. "For now, I think we really need to get going. Otherwise, we're going to be late."

I quirked an eyebrow. "Aren't you not supposed to tell me that?"

"In every version of events I've seen, me saying that didn't change what happens next."

"Is it just me," Ramsey said quietly into my ear, "or are you tired of following her orders blindly? It's almost worse knowing that we're doing something we've already done before, and we're just retracing our steps."

"I know," I groaned.

That didn't stop us from following Stacey's lead to start the trek out of nowhere and into civilization. Well, as much as New Haven could be considered civilization. It was going to take us a little while to get into town because we had to keep a low profile. Let's face it, Abram coming back into town wasn't a good idea. I didn't say anything, though, because there's no way in hell I was letting his body get away.

"All right," Huntsman said. "I think it would be best if we were not in the middle of the road all day. Maybe we should find an alternate way to get to the shelter that she"—he pointed at the woman at his side—"told us about."

I didn't understand what we were doing fully, but then again, I rarely did.

"So," I said. "Our plan is to get into New Haven, find the genie, and get her to undo the spell. Then we can handle whatever is next on the apocalypse train that Stacey is riding."

Ramsey nodded, and we started walking, leaving Huntsman to deal with the Teller.

I didn't need her to tell me where the shelter was. Growing up, we all knew about the old building that our grandparents had equipped for the end of the world. There were rumors, ghost stories, and triple-dog dares that were passed along through the younger generation to try and break into it. I rolled my eyes and led the way for Ramsey, coming up short when I heard an unintelligible screech from behind me.

"Charisse?" a familiar voice shrieked at me from a distance, completely throwing me for a loop.

After looking around until I spotted a person standing a few hundred feet away, I saw my best friend in the entire world rushing toward me with a smile on her face.

While I stood exactly where I was and let her come to me, I took in the changes that had overcome her. Lulu's hair was longer and her body was a little more thinned out than usual, but she had the same smile and her eyes held the same light they'd always had.

I'd have been thrilled to see her if Ramsey hadn't just finished telling me about how we needed to keep a low profile. Doing that was going to be hard to accomplish with Lulu knowing I was home. She wasn't exactly the wilting flower type. Most likely, by the time she got to me, half the town would know I was back.

"Oh my God!" Lulu screeched again before scooping me up into an excited hug, surprising me with her strength. I wasn't exactly light. "I didn't know you were coming back! We have to have a party! No! We have to have two parties!" She was talking so fast it was hard to keep up with her. "What the hell? Let's just throw a parade."

I shrugged when Ramsey looked at me pointedly.

Lulu's excitement was contagious, and I had to roll my eyes to keep from laughing out loud.

"It's good to see you, too, Lulu," I said, smiling and pulling away from her. "But we can't have a parade. In fact, I'm not going to be here for very long. That's why I didn't tell you I was coming. It was really a last minute, completely unplanned thing. A co-worker of mine is kind of stranded in town, and I need to find her. After that, I'll be right on my way back out. You know I don't want to overstay my welcome here."

I glanced over her shoulder and saw the people I'd come with looking at us with various degrees of curiosity.

Abram looked over at me with eyes so severe I knew he was completely disapproving of how I was handling Lulu, as though the lie wasn't completely necessary. I almost laughed. The look on his face was exactly the same look that the real Abram would have given me. He was a stickler for the truth unless a lie was absolutely necessary.

In truth, lying to Lulu was something I didn't have a choice about. We were looking for a genie who could do anything, who could look like anyone. I wasn't going to exactly say that to Lulu. Plus, a Shadow Elf had already taken over Lulu's appearance before. Who knew if a genie, or djinni, or whatever, could do the same?

Besides, it's not like Lulu could help me anyway. In order to find the genie here in New Haven, we needed to look for markers and indications of a supernatural presence; things that were out of place or impossible, events that didn't quite make sense in the context of our little town. If anyone in New Haven made sense, it was Lulu. Though I was thrilled to see her, she wasn't going to be able to help with this.

I was distracted, lost in my thoughts of what could possibly indicate where the genie was, when Lulu started talking again, and I almost missed what she was saying.

"Maybe I can help with that," Lulu was saying with an infectious grin. "Or, not me," she amended with a shrug. "I'm useless. But you should ask Ryland, for sure. She knows everything. I'm more than sure she can help you find your friend, and it wouldn't take her any time."

"Who's Ryland?" I asked, remembering that I knew basically everyone in this small town, and I'd never heard that name.

"Oh, she's the best!" Lulu said emphatically, her eyes wide and holding an excitement I wasn't sure I'd ever seen in them before. It was almost manic. "You're gonna absolutely love her!" she added, squeezing my hands and practically jumping up and down. "She's our new queen."

"What?" I asked, my heart dropping. "The new queen? Of New Haven? New Haven has a q-queen now?" I stuttered, not quite understanding what Lulu was getting at. There hadn't been any beauty queens when I lived there.

"We do!" Lulu said, chirping in delight. "Isn't it exciting? You live your whole life never knowing you needed something, and then you get it and you know that all the pieces finally fit together perfectly. I never thought we needed a queen, but since Ryland showed up, I just know that life is better with her in control. Isn't it great when fate comes in and just points a finger in the right direction?"

"It sure is, Lulu," I said, looking over at Ramsey and silently communicating what we both knew to be true, without letting on that Lulu had gone absolutely crazy.

We were looking for an odd occurrence to point the way to the genie. Something that was completely out of place.

A suburb in small-town America with its own queen and adoring followers certainly fit that bill. Especially since Lulu was the absolute last person on the planet who would ever be okay with anyone controlling her. Hell, I could remember a dozen times growing up that we'd ended up in physical fights because she wanted to be the one in control of what we did.

"Let me ask you something, Lulu." I plastered a fake smile on my face and hoped that the genie's magic was strong enough that she wouldn't know something was wrong. I tilted my head to the side and put on a mask of complete innocence and curiosity. "Is there any way my friends and I could meet the queen of New Haven?"

CHAPTER 20

"Since when did you start traveling with so many people?" Lulu mock whispered to me as we walked through the nearly abandoned streets of New Haven that led to the center of town.

She eyed the men who were no doubt here to protect me, especially from the way they kept sizing her up like she was a threat, and I had to admit...it was nice to be home. Even though we were walking, which I used to hate, I was here with the most important people in the world to me. It was nice to have a moment away from the chaos that I knew we were most likely walking into.

"I mean," she went on, "I know if I were surrounded by sexy men like that, I would be taking advantage of it."

I couldn't help but laugh softly to cover how uncomfortable her statement made me. It seemed like she didn't remember Abram or all of the things that happened before I left, and I wasn't about to poke that beehive.

"Well," I said, "you know me. I'm always looking for more people to help make me look good."

At the look of incredulousness on Ramsey's face, I shrugged and turned back to Lulu.

"Where is everyone?" I asked. "I haven't seen anyone but you since we got here." I looked around, still surprised that the entirety New Haven had been pretty much deserted.

"Oh." Lulu snickered. "Most people like to stay close to Ryland. You know, in case she has need of one of us."

I shot a concerned look at Ramsey, who was watching our interaction like a hawk. I knew him, and he would no doubt be compiling every piece of information I was able to get out of my friend. It sucked to be using her like this, but I knew something was wrong. Lulu would never just blindly accept something so outlandish like this. It was part of the reason I kept her in the dark about Abram and everything that had happened.

"Did you guys know that Char and I have been friends since we were tiny?" Lulu turned her blinding smile on Huntsman and Ramsey, seeming to ignore Abram's presence entirely. "It's true," she went on like someone had answered her. "She was even there for the birth of my daughter, saw the whole thing."

"No, I didn't," I said. "You went into labor, and I had to take you to the hospital."

Lulu snickered as we turned onto the street that her house was on. "You did more than that!" She snorted, then turned to the men again. "She was panicking and freaking out the whole time. Like I hadn't already given birth before."

She stopped talking as we came upon Lulu's large house. I stared at it, remembering an easier time. A less-complicated time, when all I needed to care about was getting my life back on track after my life as a model was over.

Ramsey stepped to my side. "Did that really happen?" He pushed up his glasses, looking a bit too comfortable with getting more dirt on me. "I mean, I can totally see that happening, but I wanted to ask for the sake of posterity."

I slapped him on the back, a bit harder than I needed to. "You know," I said quietly, "I don't think I'll tell you. But remember, when girls are best friends, they see a lot of things they don't tell men about."

With that, I left him to his own devices and took a few steps back to where Lulu was staring blankly at her house. There was something strange about it. Then I realized what.

There was nothing in her yard. No car in the driveway, no telltale sign of children, like the actual children themselves.

I mean, I didn't necessarily *like* children, but that didn't mean that I disliked them, either. Although, there was that one time that Lulu's son had run away when I was watching him and he was supposed to be taking a nap. I'd had to crawl through a hole in the fence to get him back while Lulu was losing her everloving mind.

"Hey," I said, gently touching Lulu's arm as I hesitated at the eeriness of the situation. "Where are all the toys?"

"Oh." Lulu waved me off. "There was no need to have toys in the yard. No need at all. Ryland doesn't like there to be a mess."

Abram interjected with a loud snort. "Children are supposed to make messes. That's the only thing they're good for. What's the use in having them if they're not making a mess of everything?"

Hearing him say that had me turning to face him, and I was surprised by the wistful look on his face. The moment was ruined, however, when Stacey stepped up next to him.

"Maybe," she said, "Lulu had the good sense to put the toys in the house or something. Now"—she clapped her hands and started walking away—"we've got places to go and a queen to see."

"I'm sure we'll see them later," I said. "After all, I need to give those sweet kids some Auntie Char love before we go."

Lulu grabbed my arm tightly. She was different, not the same woman who had been standing at my side only a moment ago. Her eyes were haunted, heavy with the shadows of something that I couldn't quite place. "Char."

"What's wrong, Lu?" I glanced around.

Stacey was leading the way, about thirty feet ahead of us. Abram and Huntsman were close behind her. Ramsey, on the other hand, was close enough to see us but not close enough to hear what Lulu was saying.

"They're gone," she whispered. "My husband took them away to keep them safe. To keep them away from Ryland."

In a flash, the moment with the real Lulu was over. Now, she was gone once again. In her place was the happy-go-lucky clone that had taken her place. I wiped the shocked look off my face, because there was no doubt in my mind now. The genie was here.

Ryland had a lot to answer for.

Before Lulu could ask me what I was up to, I walked away from her and got back to Ramsey's side in record time, barely winded from my rush.

"Something's wrong," I whispered, so low that I was sure nobody else but him could hear. "Lulu's kids are gone, and I think she's under the genie's spell. There was a flash," I said quickly. "Just a flash, where it was the real Lulu under there, the momma bear that she really is."

"Be prepared for anything," Ramsey answered with a small nod.

Stacey stopped up ahead. She was looking at something, but I couldn't quite make it out over Abram and Huntsman's bodies. When I got closer, I saw a sight I'd never have expected.

"Honestly," Abram said with wide eyes. "I'm not even surprised anymore. My life has been nothing but crazy since you appeared." He shook his head. "I don't know why I even bother anymore."

He stepped aside, and I was left with all of the grotesque beauty of New Haven. Okay, grotesque was the wrong word. But seriously, the entire center of town looked like it'd been pushed through a freaking wormhole and had been stuck in the Middle Ages.

The streets were cobblestone and dirt, and there were no signs of anything modern. No light poles, streetlights, signs, or electrical wires anywhere. All of the buildings looked like they'd just been built, poorly at that, and looking at the town made me want to run back to New York and take a hot shower just because I could.

Ramsey's hands balled into fists. "What am I looking at?"

"Oh God." I wheezed. "This has got to be killing you."

My laugh shocked even me.

All of our companions turned to face me, and I knew I looked like a lunatic.

"Shut up, Char," Ramsey bit out. "This isn't funny."

"You hate this shit." I clutched my stomach from laughing so hard. "After Briar, and everything she went through. Didn't you tell me that you wouldn't be caught dead anywhere near a castle again?"

"I mean it, Charisse." He took a threatening step forward, but we both knew that he wouldn't hurt me. Not only because he didn't want to, but because he was physically unable to hurt me.

Ramsey absolutely hated anything to do with castles. He hated Grimault, and he was determined not to deal with anything that even remotely reminded him of that place. Now, we walked straight into it without warning. It had to be driving him absolutely batty.

I got more laughs in, even if it was highly inappropriate. There was so much crazy going on that I needed just a moment. One moment of levity while we were surrounded by magical chaos. That's the only way I'd get through this. Finding the little things that made me laugh and exploiting them. That's how I'd always gotten through difficult situations, and I might be a completely different person than I was last time I was in New Haven, but I was still me.

REBECCA HAMILTON & CONNER KRESSLEY

I took a single step that left the modern world behind. Dirt crunched under my feet, and even the air felt different. Abram was there, taking up my personal space, in the next moment. He was close enough that I caught the musky scent that was his alone, and my body unconsciously responded.

"Be careful," he grunted.

"Why?" I snapped. "I still remember you trying to kill me."

"Well," he quipped back, "now that I've seen your body, I find that I quite like the idea of keeping it in one piece."

Huntsman joined us, his eyebrows pulled low over his eyes. "Why does this town look like it's been decimated and replaced with something two hundred years old?"

"Queen Ryland likes it this way." Lulu shrugged. "She's this way." She pointed to the large building across what I could only call a courtyard.

"Is that the nightclub?" The words slipped out, and I didn't wait for anyone else as I rushed to the doors. "Stacey," I said, "you know everything. Is this the nightclub that Abram owned?"

"Wait," Abram interjected. "I owned a nightclub? What happened to it? Was it amazing?"

I rolled my eyes and turned to the Teller. The woman was supposed to have all the answers, but she wasn't saying anything.

"Stacey," I tried again. "Tell me."

She shrugged, not saying another word, and I felt my fingers clench with the desire to hit her. I didn't, but barely. It wasn't her fault that she was only useful when I didn't actually need anything. The rest of the time, it was like owning a really big, but useless, unicorn. Which let's be real, would be cool. But still useless.

All at once, Satina's warning flooded my mind: one of these people was going to betray me.

Stacey, leading all of us through this, could definitely

count as a betrayal. Especially if she did it knowing we were going to be captured.

I shuddered with the knowledge that even as much as I wanted to trust her, to trust all of them, I couldn't. The only person I could trust was Abram, and he wasn't even the man I'd fallen in love with.

"This is it," I said, unable to keep my dejected feeling out of my voice.

There was no doubt in my mind that this was the building I'd poured my blood, sweat, and tears into. Everything I'd gone through in this building, *for* this building, everything I'd lost.

"This is the nightclub the real Abram owned," I explained to the Abram at my side. "He hired me here to fix and run it." I didn't elaborate. Didn't tell our story. That was ours, and it wasn't meant for Stacey, or Huntsman, or even Lulu to know, for that matter.

I reached to turn the handle that would lead me into the nightclub, which had been turned into something more. It was clear this was where Ryland was staying. I could feel it. Power poured off the building in waves. This was her stronghold.

It only made sense I'd have to face her here, after all. Nothing else had gone according to plan, so why would this?

The distinct click of a gun being cocked came from behind me. Instead of snapping my head around, like I wanted to, I was smart. Rule number one for facing someone with a gun: never surprise the person who has their finger on the trigger.

"I'm not armed," I said as I turned slowly. "Holy shit."

There were at least two dozen people behind us, all carrying different weapons. Where they came from, I had no idea. The roads had been completely deserted the entire time we'd been in New Haven.

Although I recognized a few faces in the crowd, none of them seemed to recognize me. Including that woman, the one who had tried to replace me as Lulu's best friend once upon a time.

"I bet I could kill half of them in the blink of an eye," Abram said to Huntsman.

Both men had matching smiles on their faces, and I took a moment to roll my eyes at their levity in this situation.

"There are people with guns," I pointed out. "Maybe you two shouldn't talk about trying to kill all of them."

I looked around while I was speaking, surprised I couldn't see Lulu anymore. She must have joined in with the crowd. I hoped she'd be safe while we were going through whatever this was.

"You could not kill more than I could." Huntsman ignored me and addressed Abram. "We could keep a tally, and the winner would win a boon from the other person."

"I'm game for that," Abram said with a shrug. "Honor system?"

"Stop," I demanded. "Neither of you is going to kill anyone. Not when we haven't found what we need."

Abram looked at me with a smile on his face. "You really aren't any fun, you know that?"

For a moment, I was transported to the beginning of our relationship.

"Well," Ramsey interrupted, "I'm only good for protecting you against these people. The genie was smart, using the community to protect herself."

"You know," Abram practically growled in my ear. "I've seen you move, although last time it was against me. If it comes to a battle, I know you can take care of yourself."

"We're innocent," Stacey said suddenly. "You wouldn't want to harm innocents who mean your queen no harm, would you?"

I stared at her, annoyed that she'd speak when she'd literally just ignored me not even five minutes before.

"I mean," I grumbled to Abram, since he was still

standing close enough to be touching, "we might mean their queen harm, if she doesn't do what we need her to."

His snort was just quiet enough to go unnoticed by the others, but I didn't miss the way his body pressed into mine. Even with everything that was happening around us, he was turned on.

"Let's go." One of the men holding the weapons prodded me with his gun.

I froze, unable to move because of the gun that was *way* too close for comfort. I hated guns on a good day, and having one touching me... Well, it was almost enough to send me into fits.

Abram growled, and the man quickly took the weapon away. Even without a weapon of his own, Abram was obviously terrifying to the smaller man. If I wasn't still traumatized from having a gun aimed at me, I might have smiled. As it was, I shrank into his side, and he put an arm around me.

The smaller man turned to the others, his face red from embarrassment. "Someone alert Queen Ryland to their presence," he ordered. "And in the meantime, take them to the dungeons."

CHAPTER 21

My foot caught, and I went down the stairs hard. Looking down as I tumbled past, I saw the same piece of wood that I thought I'd replaced when I was in charge of the nightclub. I fell, ass over teakettle, for what felt like an eternity until I hit something hard.

"Omph," was the only thing I managed to get out as I looked up slowly to see who'd caught me.

Abram, in all of his dark glory, was looking down at me with that smile. The one that said he liked the way I felt in his arms and he never wanted to let me go. His eyes devoured me, memorizing every single detail of my face.

"You've got a freckle in your eye," he said, and I was transported back to another time.

I'd fallen then, too. Right into his arms, on the day I'd met him. He was just as cocky then as he was now, but also abrasive in a way that was endearing.

"You said that to me once before." I pushed away from him, regaining my balance, and threw a glare over my shoulder at the offending step.

No one else seemed to be paying any attention to the fact I had almost broken my neck. That was probably because I was the last one down the stairs, though. By the time we rejoined the armed men, and our friends, I had my wayward emotions mostly under control.

The hallway was the exact same it'd been before the building had been burnt down by raving townspeople a few years ago. Even though it was missing the stylish furniture and accent pieces I'd found for it, I felt like I was home.

"You two," the man who'd pointed his gun at me barked. "In here." He motioned to the room he was holding a door open to, and I rolled my eyes at his idiocy.

Instead of saying anything, I swept past him with my head held high and walked into the dungeon. It wasn't an actual dungeon, though, surprising not only me but Abram as well. His grunt of appreciation made me smile.

"At least they thought of a bed," he said as he sat down on the full-sized frame that sat in the center of the room.

The door slammed shut behind me, and the lock clicked into place.

"Well." Abram smiled. "You're stuck with me now, lass. What do you plan to do about it?"

"Oh my." I played along by placing a hand on my hip and sashaying as I walked closer. "I honestly don't know." I bit my lip and then ran my tongue over it, smiling as I saw the way his eyes flared while he watched.

He reached for me, seeming almost unconsciously, and I laughed.

"There's not enough time in the day for me to tell you how many ways that *won't* be happening."

There was a large chair a few feet away, so I detoured for it. Abram watched me go, the appreciation in his eyes shifting to something else. Almost like suspicion, but different. I stared at him, unable to look away before he did. The last time we were in a room like this, he'd been naked.

As if he'd heard my thoughts, he smiled devilishly. "You know," Abram said. "I'd be happy to have a repeat performance. Even if you don't want to talk about it…I know you felt it, too."

He was right, and I was tired of being dishonest. "Do you know," I told him, "the first time we had sex was in this building?"

"I didn't know that," he admitted. "Is there something special about it? Other than the fact I owned it, that is."

The muscles in his arms rippled as he crossed them across his chest. He was making himself comfortable on the bed, and my body was beginning to ache with the need to join him.

My brain knew better, though. Knew that this wasn't *my* Abram. But my body was a completely different story. By the time my gaze made it to his face, he was watching me hungrily. The passion there wasn't masked by anything.

"Well?" he pressed.

I coughed. "No. There's nothing special about the building. It was us, together. That was it."

"I know." Abram cocked an eyebrow. "I felt it during the spell. Not all of it, not all at once. Pieces, like I wasn't supposed to get my hands on them. Fragments of a life with you I sure as hell don't remember. That's why it changed my truth. It was the first time in my memory that I wanted something. Really wanted something, and you were there in front of me. Abram, the other Abram, is a lucky man."

The honesty in his words was enough to strike a wound deep in my chest. He wasn't supposed to be like this. He wasn't supposed to be sweet. This man was supposed to be dark and the opposite of the man I loved.

"Stop," I said quietly. "You aren't him."

"I never claimed to be him," Abram said. "But somewhere along the line, you're going to have to accept that he's not here. I am."

"I'm your weakness," I blurted. "His and yours, and I've known it since the night we met again. You wanted to kill me.

You thought about it. But you couldn't do it," I said fiercely. "Do you know why?"

He stood from the bed and took a step toward me, no doubt trying to be intimidating. He wasn't, though, not to me. Just like always, I wasn't afraid of his beast; I never could be.

"It's that beast inside you," I told him.

Somewhere in the past thirty seconds, I'd grown a thousand percent tired of dealing with him on uneven footing. I missed Abram. I missed him being there, and the small little nuances of this Abram were driving me crazy.

I went on, unable to stop. "The beast that you struggled to contain around me that night. He belongs to me. He has my entire life. From the time he swore to my father that he would keep me safe, until now. Even now, your beast would rather die than hurt me, I guarantee it."

Where this burst of confidence was coming from, I had zero clue. I wasn't going to stop here, though. Abram wanted to push me, so I was going to push him right back and prove my point while I was at it.

"You should try to hurt me, Abram." I felt calm. Probably more calm than I should be while I was poking the beast. "See what I am saying is true for yourself."

I got up, and took a step closer to him when it looked like he was going to step back. There was fear in his eyes. Real fear, something I hadn't seen since the day I lost Abram to the darkness inside him.

"Take me by the throat, Abram. Try and squeeze the life out of me."

"No," he choked out. "I've got no reason to kill you."

"Prove my point, Abram," I goaded him. "You know it irritates you that I have this much power over you. That I'm your weakness."

He shook his head furiously. "Not gonna happen, Sweet Cheeks."

That was it. I let the magic go, as much as I could, without letting him know what I was doing. My fingers flexed and my magic wound its way through his body, tightening itself on his hands and his heart.

In the next moment, Abram's fangs slipped out, revealing the beast inside that wanted to break free.

"Now," I snarled, getting in his face.

He didn't say a word as he struggled to fight the magic I'd cast. I knew it was coming, but it still shocked the shit out of me when he grabbed me by the throat and lifted me off the ground. I was two feet in the air, easy, and dangling. I grabbed at his hands, but he squeezed a little tighter.

"See what you made me do," he said with a deceptively calm voice. "I told you no, but you had to go and push me. Now, I'll have no choice but to hurt you."

"You won't hurt me." I gasped through the smallest of openings in my windpipe. I choked the next moment as heat rose in my face. I couldn't breathe, let alone speak anymore.

"Abram." I closed my eyes as I tried to get the words out.

His lips pressed against mine, and the hold on my throat loosened. Immediately I gulped for air, and his tongue forced its way into my mouth. For a moment, the briefest of seconds, I returned his kiss. As soon as I came to my senses, I bit his lip and pulled away.

I scurried back to the chair, doing my best not to let him see my fear. I almost thought he would hurt me.

"Char." He took a step forward, but I stopped him with a hand in the air.

"You. Are. Not. Him."

"I haven't been for a long time, Ms. Bellamy!" he roared. "Don't you see that I know that?"

His words brought me up short. No one, no one except *my* Abram, called me that.

His chest was heaving, and his eyes were downcast. His hair was a mess, and he wasn't facing me. I shouldn't have known, but I did.

"It's you," I whispered.

Seconds ticked by, and I took a step toward him when he didn't move to answer me. I was shaking, and I couldn't tell if it was from him choking me or the realization that it was really him. Really *my* Abram.

"Once upon a time," I said. "I fell in love with a beast."

His head jerked up, and I saw it. He was there, in those eyes. My Abram.

"I don't know how long I have with you, Char."

"I know."

I was going to have him. I didn't care about the time, or the fact that his replacement had just choked me. I needed Abram. I needed his touch. I threw myself at him, knowing that Abram would never let me fall. He didn't, either. Two hands under my ass held me to him, and my legs wrapped around his waist. The arousal I'd done my damndest to ignore only a few minutes before was pressing into me, and I had to touch it.

With my lips pressed against his, and his tongue exploring my mouth like he'd never kissed me before, I let my hands wander. Down his chest and to his pants. I loosened his belt while Abram moved us to the bed, never breaking the kiss. Once I had his pants undone, I reached inside, knowing that what I would find would make my world complete.

His cock was there immediately, jutting out proudly. I touched his head, and I felt the precum leaking. I groaned, and Abram swallowed it with his own moan.

I broke the kiss to say, "Now. I can't wait."

He turned and dropped me onto the bed. I kicked off my shoes, and reached for my top to pull it over my head. Abram went for my pants, and in less than ten seconds, I was completely bare to him. While he admired the view, I spread my legs and played with myself while climbed onto the bed.

Soon, he was pressing his hard cock to my entrance, and I

threw my head back with the pleasure and pain of him filling me with one thrust.

"So. Tight." He swore. "Why are you so tight?"

"It's been a year," I told him. "Nothing feels as good as you, so I haven't even bothered." I was breathless, and that was about the last thing I said before I started to fall off the first of hopefully many peaks.

"No," he demanded. "Not yet. If you go, I'm going to blow. I can't have that happen yet."

Abram slowed his pace, thrusting as deep as he could with every pass, and he pressed his lips to my forehead. I didn't care that the world was ending around us. I didn't care about Huntsman, or Stacey, or even Ramsey. I cared about Abram, filling me completely and refusing to let me go without him.

"Abram," I whined. "Please. I need this."

He stopped, his chest heaving and his eyes clenched shut. I cried out as he pulled completely out, and he pressed a kiss to my lips.

"You'll cum first, don't worry."

When his lips pressed to first one nipple and then the other, my back arched. He wasn't done, though. His hands caressed my body, and his mouth went farther down until he was at my core. His tongue darted out, and he pressed two fingers deep inside me.

"Abram!" I cried out.

His chuckle against my thigh was almost as erotic as the fingers he was moving inside me, bring nme quickly back to that edge.

I screamed as I climaxed, and I felt Abram suck at my clit until there was nothing I could do but moan and writhe in pleasure.

"Look at me," he ordered.

I opened my eyes, barely able to function at this point, and he smiled.

"You're mine."

I nodded. "Always."

"Good." He filled me again, and if it weren't impossible, I'd say he'd grown in size.

I was full, so full. Every single thrust brought me closer to another orgasm. He wasn't gentle now. No, he was owning me, marking me as his. It was too much and not enough.

"I'm there again," I said through the haze.

I barely got the words out before I was pushed over the cliff and into another orgasm. This time Abram finished with me. He pulled out completely, though, and he used his hand to rub his cum into my skin, marking me in a primal way.

"Why'd you do that?" I asked.

"So that when he comes back, he knows that he may have my body, but I own your soul."

I reached for him, needed the kiss that his lips offered. One moment, he was there with me, kissing me with everything he had. The next, he faltered and pulled back.

"Char?" He looked down at where our naked bodies were pressed together, and his eyes clouded over.

"He's gone," I said quietly. "Already."

"I tried," Not Abram said. "I tried to give him as much time as I could, but I was forced back."

I pushed away, feeling desolate as I pulled a blanket over my body to cover my nakedness.

I'd just had sex with the man I loved, and he was still here. But it wasn't him. It would never be him, not forever.

Confusion and guilt crashed into me. Was sleeping with Abram wrong? I would have regretted passing on a chance at intimacy with the man I loved, not knowing when or if the chance would ever present itself again. But the rushed sex left me feeling cold.

When Not Abram turned around, I got dressed and slipped my shoes back on. Out of the corner of my eye, I saw Abram doing the same.

"Charisse," he said comfortingly. "I know you don't want

to hear this. I saw everything. I may be crass, and I may be a dick. But I would never…you know."

The sob escaped before I could stop it, and I was angrier than I'd been in a long time. The tears were supposed to be done. I wasn't supposed to cry about this anymore.

He reached for me. "Charisse."

Before he could touch me, the door to our cell opened, and the same man from before was standing there with a knowing smile on his face. He turned to the unmade bed and sniffed the air.

"Well," he said. "I suppose I missed all the fun."

Abram took a step forward and snarled, but I stopped him with a hand on his arm.

"He's not worth it," I told him.

"Let's go," the man said. "I've got orders to bring you upstairs."

He moved to grab my arm, but I stepped around him. Abram tried to follow, but the door was shut in his face and locked again. When I looked at the man with a gun for an answer, he just shrugged.

"You're the only one wanted," he said by way of explanation. "You know, it really is admirable how many men you carry around with you. First, you've got three men with you, and now, the queen's right-hand man wants to see you. I'm surprised. Especially because of how fat you are."

I clenched my hands into fists. I'd been hearing I was fat half my life. I wasn't about to let this idiot goad me.

"Well," I told him with a false smile, "I guess they just like curves."

He didn't say another word as he led me up through the building to where the offices used to be. I followed closely, not wanting to give him a reason to point his gun at me again.

"Through there." The man pointed to an open door, and I walked into the room beyond with as much courage as I could muster.

"Well, well," a voice I hadn't heard in years said from the darkness. It was a voice that couldn't be here. It was impossible. I'd killed him.

Dalton walked toward me, the shadows leaving his face, and a hard look in his eyes.

"Fuck," I muttered and ran for the door.

Before I could even take a step outside, he was there with one hand wrapped in my hair. He yanked me back and slammed the door shut, closing me off from any chance of escape.

"You're not going anywhere, Charisse."

CHAPTER 22

DALTON WAS SQUEEZING SO HARD that flashes of light danced in front of my eyes. The lack of oxygen was taking its toll, and I couldn't breathe more than a gasp at a time. It hurt so badly, and I couldn't even get my magic to respond.

Scratching at him, kicking didn't seem to faze him in the slightest. In an instant, he'd stripped me of the strength I'd gained since we last saw one another. I was helpless, the same woman who'd almost lost everything.

"Dalton," I choked, the word barely audible over the alarms blaring inside my skull. "Stop."

His muscles had to be straining with the effort of holding me up. The thought flickered through my mind as everything grew dim.

My eyes closed, and I knew if he didn't stop, I was going to pass out any second now.

He didn't answer at first. Didn't acknowledge my fingers scratching against his hands, though the grip he had on my throat lightened minutely. Just enough to keep me alive. Air rushed into my lungs, and I coughed from trying to take such a sudden deep breath.

A smile cracked across Dalton's face. He was just as demented as I remembered.

"I remember everything you did to me, you know." His once attractive face contorted in rage. "You killed me, Charisse. You took away my chance at forever. Now, I don't even have my power as a beast. At least you still have your magic to keep you warm at night. I've been surviving off Ryland's scraps."

Dalton was dead. He couldn't be here. I'd killed him. He was seriously the only person I'd actively *tried* to kill.

"I chopped off your head," I said dumbly.

I really had. I'd watched it separate from his body. I'd had nightmares about it constantly after it happened. Abram held me through the tears, telling me that I did the right thing. I knew for a fact that he'd been dead.

The way his eyes flared at my words told me that I'd made a mistake. As though his grip tightening against my throat wasn't enough. I tried to get away, but it wasn't working. My magic still wasn't responding. I flexed so hard that I thought it'd explode out of me, but nothing. Not even a wisp of magic left my fingers.

"I could spill every ounce of your blood," Dalton whispered against my face. "Do you think if I did, I might be able to get my power back?"

He was crazy. Even crazier than he'd been before.

"No," I croaked.

He wasn't squeezing my throat hard enough to kill me anymore. Just hard enough that it was extremely uncomfortable to breathe, and I couldn't take a full breath, either.

"Shame." His eyes flashed. "Ryland wants you alive for now, for some godforsaken reason, but I think you'd be better off dead, just like the beast you were with. I can smell him on you. You disgust me, Charisse Bellamy."

He'd played his hand, though. Hurting me was one thing,

but Dalton's boss wanted me alive. That knowledge gave me a hint of strength, and I met Dalton's snarl with a smile.

"You know," I said. "He took me in that bed. In the dungeon you put us in. I wonder how much that hurts, Dalton. To know that no matter what you did, or what you do, you'll never be the beast I need to keep my bed warm at night."

"You know that he won't be able to give you forever, Charisse. He won't live long enough. No beast could survive that mark on their chest. Not for long. It's too bad, really. I'd love another chance to kill him."

Dalton's words made me sick to my stomach. I pulled back, trying to get out of his hold. He didn't budge, though.

"Fuck," I grunted. "Let me go."

He laughed in my face, spittle landing on my skin as he did.

"No." He caressed my cheek, in a twisted version of affection. "Once Ryland is done with you, I'm going to kill your beast the way you killed me."

Threatening me didn't do it. Physically assaulting me didn't, either. It was the very real threat to Abram that woke up my magic. I didn't even have a chance to cast the spell before power was flying from my fingertips. I couldn't control it, and I didn't want to. Not when I was faced with Dalton and everything he wanted to do to me, *had* done to me.

Dalton had been choking me, threatening Abram, and nowthen his mouth was sealed shut. There was only skin where his mouth had been a few seconds before. His hands slipped from around my throat, and I landed on both feet with a soft thud, while Dalton collapsed next to me. His hands covered most of his face, so it took a few seconds for me to see exactly what I'd done to him.

Horror and fascination warred in my mind as I stepped over him, seeing the handiwork my power had manifested.

Dalton couldn't breathe. That much was clear. His face

was red, and he was scratching at himself. His nose, his lips, even his ears were all sealed shut. It was as if I'd taken an eraser and eliminated those parts of his anatomy. He was suffocating, and there was nothing I wanted to do to help him.

He used to be handsome, in a boy-next-door sort of way. Now, though, I could barely tell that he was human. Not with the way his skin looked like it was melting in on itself. Most definitely not with the way his face was drenched in blood. His fingers were covered in it, and he was pleading for help with his eyes. I'm sure the moaning he was doing behind his sealed mouth was his last ditch effort to get me to break the spell.

"You hurt me," I said slowly, staring into his bulging eyes. "Not only that, but you're going to try and hurt the man I love. You deserve to die, just like you did the first time. You murdered women, and you tried to murder me. Goodbye, Dalton. I hope you stay dead this time."

I could still feel where his hands had wrapped around my throat, and there would no doubt be bruises there for a long time. Dalton was dying, again. This time, I wouldn't see his blood pooling around his corpse. Sometime in the past year or more, I'd grown bloodthirsty. I wanted to see his blood, to make sure that he couldn't come back and haunt me.

When he reached out to grab my leg, I stepped out of his reach and smiled. Yes, I felt like a crazy person, but I wasn't about to leave until I was sure that Dalton was dead. Again. The last bits of movement stopped, and his lifeless eyes stared up at the ceiling.

"Finally," I muttered.

Just for good measure, I kicked Dalton's corpse. Then I turned to the closed door that led to the nightclub-turned-castle. It was a lot. Too much, really. But I didn't have a choice. I never had a choice. Beyond that door were a hundred different things I needed to do, people I needed to find, and a genie I had to force back into a bottle.

Knowing exactly what was next, I turned the handle on the door and stepped into the hall.

Empty. There absolutely nothing out here. I closed the door silently behind me, not sparing a glance for Dalton. The halls around me were silent, and I tried my best not to make a sound as I headed back toward the basement. My first stop needed to be getting my friends out of their cells. *Then* we could find the genie.

The stairs creaked as I stepped down them, but I kept going, breathing a sigh of relief when I made it to the bottom and no one appeared. There was something weird about being back in New Haven that was making my magic unstable, and I didn't want to get caught unprepared by any crazy people waving weapons around.

"Do you think we're safe now?" Stacey's voice filtered from one of the rooms, and I paused before trying to open the door.

I don't know why--call it an obsession with proving that she didn't know absolutely *everything* that was going to happen--but I had to hear what she was saying.

"We must be." Huntsman's voice caught me by surprise. "After all, the queen summoned her. I heard the way that other one, the one that used to be a beast, left with her."

"Good. That means she'll be gone soon, and this nightmare will be over."

I couldn't believe my ears. What was Stacey talking about? And why was Huntsman part of it?

When I reached for the handle to call them on their bullshit and find out what was happening, another person joined the conversation. Someone I never should have heard.

"I still don't understand why we had to wait all this time." Briar's annoyingly sweet voice filtered through the door. "It took you guys long enough to get her here."

What the hell?

I clapped my hand over my mouth so that they couldn't so much as hear me breathe.

"You know why," Huntsman said. "We were looking for the best path forward."

"Hmm," Briar said. "I thought it was going to be harder for Ramsey to get her back to New Haven, though. She keeps talking about how much she hates it. But it barely took any effort at all. Just a fake spell, and she came running."

Ramsey's laugh had me falling to my knees. Oblivious to anyone who might sneak up on me, I let the pain of their betrayal wash through me. All of them. I didn't need to see their faces to know it was true, either. I'd spent so much time the last few days listening to Stacey, I could tell just by the inflection that it was her. And Ramsey had been my constant companion over the past year, which meant I'd spent more than enough time with Briar since the two were often together.

"Lulu," Ramsey said, "I'm sorry for the sacrifices you had to make to help us get to this point, but I hope it's worth the result in the end."

Lulu laughed, and I felt the very last bit of my heart shatter into a million pieces.

"It wasn't anything at all," she said. "Knowing this nightmare is almost over, it's enough to make me do just about anything."

I listened to them, unable to move or defend myself. I was stuck while the people I cared about the most proved to me that I was alone.

"I can't believe it's almost done." Lulu broke through the haze of pain that had descended over my head. "Once Char is dead, my family can come back. That's what Ryland promised me. A small price to pay."

I crept forward on my hands and knees. I was sure that I couldn't stand, not with how much it physically hurt to hear this. But I needed to get closer. I needed to face them, to see their reaction once they realized that I knew they'd betrayed me. Only after I saw them with my own eyes would I be able to figure out what to do next.

My heart raced, and I crept forward until I was sure that they would hear me shuffling around. No one appeared, though. I held my breath for a few seconds, trying to steady my heart while I attempted to use my magic to shield me. Thankfully, it obeyed, and I felt the steady pulsing that indicated I should be okay. I wasn't going to take any chances, though. I stayed low and kept as quiet as possible. After all, as much as I might hate him right now, Ramsey was an extremely powerful mage.

The door was hanging ajar, barely. I stuck my face right up to it, down low, and saw my worst fear. It really was them. Some part of me had hoped seeing in the room would prove some other possibility. Reveal that it was all just a trick. But there was no way that the genie could impersonate all of them at the same time.

There was no sign that there was anything wrong with them. Huntsman and Stacey stood side by side. Ramsey held Briar in his arms, his lips pressed against her cheek. Lulu stood alone, and she was still smiling. The only one I didn't see was Abram. It didn't change anything, though. Seeing them here, it decimated every piece of the trust I had for any of them.

Even the way Huntsman was staring at Stacey hurt. Instead of the annoyed distance that he'd had since the moment she introduced herself, he was eating her up with his eyes. While I stared, he reached over and brushed her hair behind her ear. It was clear that I was missing more than just a few of the pieces.

"I wish I had a chance to say goodbye," Lulu said suddenly, looking away from the others. "It sucks that Char has to die to save the rest of us. Are we sure this is the right thing? There's nothing else we can do?"

That comment hurt worst of all. It meant that Lulu did care about me, or had at some point. Just not enough to stand by what was right.

At least Abram wasn't there with them. There was a chance that he wasn't involved. He couldn't be. My mind raced with the possibilities and shifting plans. I had to get away. Screw the rest of them. I'd get to Abram, and the two of us could get the hell away from here. If Huntsman was part of this, there was no reason for me to help him.

Shuffling backward, awkwardly since I was still crouched down, I practically waddled to get away without them hearing or seeing me. I was almost safe when I heard shuffling from behind me.

"What are you doing out here?"

I shrieked, and fell forward. My head slammed into the door, and I ended up sprawled on the floor in front of the people who had betrayed me. I kept my eyes shut, refusing to look at them, refusing to cry for any of the things that they'd just said about me. I couldn't stand to see the looks on their faces.

Thankfully, it was completely silent. No doubt they were shocked that I'd ended up there, listening to their private conversation. Especially when they'd been talking about how I was going to die. My life seriously couldn't get any worse.

Bootsteps stopped right at my head, and I held my breath with fear that someone was going to hurt me. I opened one eye, and the barrel of a gun was pointed directly at my face, again.

"Queen Ryland is ready to see you now. No more games, Charisse."

CHAPTER 23

I STARED at the man who was supposed to be my friend. The one who was supposed to guide me in this whole messed up world. Ramsey, as a mage, shouldn't be able to actually shoot me. But then, what if that had been just another lie he'd told me? What if mages really could hurt others?

"Ramsey." The name came out like acid. "Was everything we've gone through in the past year a lie? Did none of it matter?"

Ramsey stopped, and when I kept walking, he reached out and touched my arm. I recoiled, not wanting to even have that minor touch between the two of us. He wasn't my friend.

"You don't understand," he said, his expression crestfallen. "If we hadn't gone to investigate Ryland's magic, none of this would have happened. We'd be safe."

"Is that when you betrayed me, then? Are you trying to say everything up until this week was the truth, and one genie was able to convince you to turn against me after everything we've been through? After everything I've done for you?" I slapped his hand away as he leaned toward me again. I knew he was just trying to calm me down, but I was so far beyond that. So far beyond anything he could possibly say to make this better.

"I bought Briar tampons because you were too chicken to do it."

Ramsey's face looked ravaged. "It's not like that."

Honestly, up until that moment, I had hope that it was one bad trick. That I'd find out that all of it was a lie. That look, though. I knew every single one of Ramsey's expressions. It was a side effect of training and working together like we had for as long as we had. This is the one that told me he was telling the truth. He'd betrayed me. He was throwing me to the wolves, or in this case, the genie.

My shoulders slumped. "What happened?"

"She appeared as soon as the spell took root," he said quietly.

He leaned against the wall. I took in every inch of his body and his movements. The way his muscles flinched when they came into contact with the cold stone that lined the hall. I saw the way his eyes held the weight of the world, and how even his fingers seemed to twitch with the desire to make everything go back to the way it had been.

"Tell me all of it," I demanded. There was no venom in my voice, no anger. Just resentment that he'd done something I would never be able to forgive.

"She appeared as though she'd been summoned." Ramsey looked down at his hands, clearly ashamed of what he was confessing. "Not even Huntsman was able to stop her. She told us about the future, what we were all going to lose. She showed me what happened to Briar, to our family. All of it because we wouldn't surrender you. She told us that you were the target. That in order to save everyone else, we had to sacrifice you."

"This isn't *Heroes*," I said. "You can't just sacrifice one person to save the rest." My hands balled into fists, and I struggled to get a handle on my emotions.

Ramsey was shaking his head, though. "Yes," he said

determinedly. "She's bound by the laws of magic, Charisse. She's not able to lie, not when she's in her true form."

I snorted. "You're so sure it was her true form?"

"There's more," he went on. "The reason that we couldn't tell you. The reason that we had to come back to New Haven."

"What?" I scoffed. "What's so important about this place?"

"You haven't changed that much." Ramsey shrugged and met my stare. "You would burn the world down to save Abram, to bring him back to you. In this place, you remember what putting him first does. What it has done to your family. To your friends."

Ramsey's words sank in like the well-placed blow they were. They dug deep into my soul and refused to let go. He was right. I really would sacrifice everything else to have Abram back.

"We could have fought whatever this is," I told him. "We could have done this together. Remember that." I cursed. "You did this. Not me. I never want to see you, or any of them, ever again."

The pain was too much, and I knew I'd never forgive him for this.

I was too busy wiping my eyes, trying to keep the tears from falling down my cheeks. I didn't hear anyone approach.

"I thought I told you to bring her to me."

I jumped, turning to face the person behind the sugary-sweet voice. She was stunning, but there was no mistaking the fact that she was Ryland, the genie. Her long black hair was bound around her head, with pieces hanging down her back. Her skin was tan, like she'd spent her entire life playing in the sun.

But it was her eyes that gave her away. They were bright purple, and even though she was wearing a smile, I knew that she would just as soon slit my throat and walk away. Her dress, though, was something I would have worn in my days as a model. It was pale lavender, with black lace detailed into the hem, and skintight, hugging every one of her curves. She wasn't as full-figured as I was, but she had curves that most women would kill for. Not only was her appearance a dead giveaway that she was supernatural, but so was the fact that I could feel her magic coursing over my skin.

I rolled my eyes and sniffed to cover up that I'd been fighting tears. "Queen Ryland, I presume." The sassiness was real, and there was no way I could control it at this point, so I wasn't even going to try.

"That's me, Charisse Bellamy." She turned to Ramsey and dismissed him without saying a word.

He practically scurried down the hall, without so much as a glance over his shoulder to make sure I was okay. Just one more thing to add to the pile of hurt.

"Follow me." Ryland spun on heels I hadn't realized she was wearing. She flounced through a doorway, and I followed, determined to learn everything I could and fight to the end.

"So," I said to cover being so far out of my league it wasn't funny. "You're a genie. Like from the children's movie." It wasn't a question, and she likely saw it for the insult it was meant to be.

Ryland twirled her long hair around a slender finger. "Do you know what a genie is capable of?"

"Nope," I said with a pointed look around. "I don't have a clue. Oh." I snapped my fingers. "I know. You can turn friends against one another." I ticked a finger. "You can transport the entire town a hundred years into the past." One more finger down. "You can bring people back from the dead."

The genie's laugh stopped before I could spit more vitriol at her.

"What?" I snapped. "You think it's funny?"

Ryland snickered before she wiped her eyes and waved to a small coffee table that sat in the center of the room between two chairs. I glanced around, taking a moment to see what I hadn't noticed when I walked in. I was surrounded by a huge, marble expanse. There wasn't a throne, though.

"Do you know what impresses me about you, Charisse?" Ryland smiled at me when I looked at her again. "The fact that you think this is me." She waved a hand around her.

"What are you talking about?"

"Everything, and I do mean everything that I know about you, told me that you would forgive your friends for their betrayal. And yet, now I'm not so sure. You continue to surprise me, and that is hard to do after hundreds of years trapped in a bottle."

I looked at her, the genie, and I saw something I didn't think I'd see. I saw a human side to her. She was supposed to be a monster. A creature that I could condemn back to the bottle to save Huntsman. That plan had been shot to shit, though. I didn't have a plan anymore, and I really didn't have anyone to blame for that.

With a sigh, I took a seat at the table Ryland had motioned to earlier. Defeated, I waited for her to join me.

"I'm impressed by you," Ryland admitted. "Your propensity for forgiveness extends to a man who you love with every fiber of your being even though he's not that man. Yet the friends who have stood by you through your darkest moments, you will not forgive."

I shook my head. "You wouldn't understand. You're not human."

As soon as I said the words, I regretted them. Why? I had no clue. But I could tell they hurt. Thinking quickly, I decided to go all in. If I was going to die, I might as well inflict damage any way I could.

"You sent a shadow monster after me," I said bluntly. "You did all of this. I never did anything to you, and I wouldn't have even known you existed except for the fact that you came after me. Now, you're going to try and kill me."

I huffed. Saying that, putting the words out there into the world, took the air from my sails. It was really happening. Not just something I could wish away.

"I'm not going to kill you," Ryland said. "I was never going to kill you. That wasn't my plan. If I *had* wanted to kill you, you'd be dead. It wasn't easy to trap Huntsman. None of this was easy, especially with how volatile you are."

She sat down, and everything shifted. The cold marble room that we'd been in changed, taking on the appearance of a warm and inviting kitchen. It looked like *my* kitchen actually. The only thing that was missing were my ridiculous decorations.

"I thought this might make you feel a little bit more comfortable," Ryland said. "Maybe if you're comfortable, you'll give me a chance to tell you what you're not understanding because you're so stubborn."

Immediately, my back tensed even more than I thought was possible. "I'm not stubborn," I insisted while shaking my head. "You don't know what you're talking about."

My refusal just made Ryland laugh, which made me angrier. We weren't getting anywhere, and I was losing time. Time that I needed to figure out my next step. To figure out how to stop her. Although, I didn't know why I cared anymore.

"If you're not going to kill me," I said, "does that mean I can leave?"

She shook her head, and my hopes were dashed. "Charisse, there's a reason I summoned you here. Unfortunately, your friends were the only way to get you here. If I could have done so without the need for them to betray you, I would have. Believe me."

Her words, and the way she looked at me when she said them... There was something I wasn't understanding, something I should be able to piece together.

"New Haven is the epicenter of the magical storm that

even you know has been on the horizon for over a year now," Ryland continued. "You're needed here now, where your magic has wreaked the most havoc."

"My magic?" I laughed. "I didn't do any of this. You did." I looked around. "I had nothing to do with any of this."

"Of course you did." Ryland's eyes shone with laughter, and she started to tap her fingers on the table that sat between us. "None of what's happening in New Haven has anything to do with me. I just followed the massive amounts of power that were seeping out. When I got here, I found a town that was seriously out of whack. Plus, there was a crazy man walking around talking about how you'd murdered him."

Dalton. She was talking about Dalton. Plus, she was saying that none of this had to do with her.

"That doesn't make any sense," I mumbled. "I'm not powerful enough for this."

Everything was wrong, so wrong.

"I didn't bring Dalton back to life. I didn't send New Haven back in time. I didn't do any of this."

"Charisse," Ryland said.

I looked up at her, and she reached across the table to place her hand on top of mine.

"I know that you've been doubting yourself the past year," she said. "But you're the *only* conduit who is also a supplicant. You're the only Dual that I've ever heard of. You're the only person in the world who I know could ever be powerful enough to do something like this." She waved a hand needlessly around the room.

"You're wrong," I said.

"I'm not," Ryland said with pity in her voice. "Your worst nightmares… I saw them after I sent the Shadow Elf to you. Dalton, his murder, haunted your dreams for a year. New Haven, the way the townspeople acted like they were straight out of the past. The way they hunted and hurt Abram. These things came from you, from the power that you can't control."

I groaned. "No."

My hands shook, my heart raced, and my head pounded against my skull. I deflated. Physically and emotionally. I couldn't do this.

"Don't do that," Ryland commanded. "Do not doubt yourself. You're the only one who anyone in power seems to want. Hell—" She laughed. "—they want you so badly that they're offering me my freedom in exchange for me bringing you this letter and seeing the completion of their contract."

"What?" I looked down at the table, where there was a piece of parchment paper I hadn't seen before. "What is that?"

"That's the best offer you're ever going to get. I hope you take it. Because if you don't, the power flowing through your veins is going to keep growing out of control. It's going to destroy you, and it's going to destroy everything you've ever touched."

"How do you know that?" I touched the parchment, and there was something familiar about the handwriting scrawled over the top of it.

"Because The Brothers told me that the only way to fix this is for you to choose. I just hope you make the right decision, because the fate of the world lies in your hands."

CHAPTER 24

I OPENED the letter from The Brothers with trembling fingers, unable to stop the trickle of fear that slid down my spine. Ryland had put the weight of the world on my shoulders, literally, as I read the words addressed to me.

DEAR MS. BELLAMY,

It has come to our attention that you are displeased with the current state of affairs in your life. While we understand and certainly sympathize with your plight, we regret to inform you that there is only one way for you to resolve your predicament.

You were warned, through various means, of the danger we might bring to your life. You made the conscientious decision to ignore these warnings. As a result, we have sent an emissary to guarantee that you will listen to reason.

We, of course, are aware you have no desire to listen to what your current options are. As a result, we have chosen to take away every other avenue you might have. The only way to save yourself from destruction, our dear Ms. Bellamy, is to go back to before you discovered your magical ties.

As you can see, your only option is to give up your life of magic and return to the mundane existence that was your life. Your friends have betrayed you, and would rather sacrifice you than suffer the fate that we have in store for them.

We hope you will find it within yourself to come to terms with your new situation. Our emissary has the power to grant your wish, as it were. Provide her with your answer posthaste, and have your greatest wish granted. Of course, by that, we imply that you will take the only chance you'll find to go home.

Go home, Ms. Bellamy, and live a life free of magic.

While we wish you well, we hope never to speak again.

The Company

"You're kidding me, right?" I stared down at the letter, hoping that I was hallucinating. "You're going to send me back in time? If you have the power to do that, why are we going through all of this in the first place?"

Ryland, with a grace that I should have expected from her, shrugged and then patted my hand. She smiled and shook her head at me the way a mother might while dealing with a ridiculous child.

"Think about it, Charisse." She tapped the letter I was still clenching in my hands. "On my own? Not a chance in hell I'd be able to send you back. The Brothers? They're the ones with the power. They're the ones who are going to send you back. But even they can only do so if you wish for it yourself."

"I doubt they'd do anything to help me," I mused.

"They're not." Ryland laughed. "The Brothers only ever do anything to help themselves. Anything that comes off as altruistic is only because they want it to seem that way, to get the results they need with the least resistance possible. They're not so bad, though. There have definitely been worse men in power in my long life."

"Yeah." I scoffed. "If you're so sure they're not bad, then

why would they send you to convince my friends to betray me?"

"What would you rather have, Charisse? Would you know the truth of your situation, or would you bury your head in the sand for another year? Would you fight a pointless battle, one that you have no hope of winning? Or would you rather go back to a time when you were happy?"

"I—I—You don't—" I shook my head, as if that would help the words come, but I didn't know what to say.

I wanted to argue that I was happy, that I *am* happy. I couldn't, though. She was right, and it was time to face the fact that I didn't have anyone in my corner. Not anymore.

But how far back could they send me? Till before my mom died? Would she die again? Would The Brothers ensure I never crossed paths with Abram? And could I bring myself to make that choice?

"Do you want to see something?" Ryland asked, smiling at me like there was nothing wrong. Like I wasn't going through monumental discoveries about myself.

"What?" I laced my fingers together and pressed the heels of my palms together, needing to feel something real. Needing the minor comfort it offered. "What do you want to show me?"

The look on her face told me two things: one, she was sympathetic to whatever I was going through, which made it harder to hate her on the principle of what she'd done to me. And two, she was just as mischievous as Stacey was, and that meant I had no clue what would happen next. As it turned out, I really had no idea what was going to happen at all.

She squealed and then clapped her hands together. "This is going to be fun."

Everything shifted, and I was left feeling majorly disoriented. Frantic, I grabbed the edge of the table, trying to steady myself. My hands fell to my sides, though. The table was gone, and everything vanished in a cloud of bright purple smoke.

I gasped. "What the hell?"

Ryland's smile, now purely mischievous, vanished along with the rest of her. I tried to run. To get away, to use my power to break whatever spell she was casting, but I was stuck. I should have known I wasn't safe.

The room around me spun, and I closed my eyes, trying to find even the slightest bit of relief from the chaos surrounding me.

My stomach rolled. Wind whipped around me, my hair slapping me in the face no matter how much I tried to keep it tamed. I was stuck in the middle of a hurricane, right in the center of the throne room of Ryland's castle.

I kept my eyes closed, not wanting to lose the little bit of food in my stomach. Just as quickly as the wind and destruction started, it stopped. One second, it was loud, rushing through my hair, feeling as though I were flying through the air, and the next, everything was silent.

Shocked I was still alive, I opened my eyes. Then I blinked several times, because it was like I'd stepped onto another planet. Okay, maybe not another planet, but definitely somewhere far from New Haven.

My eyes jumped from color to color, overwhelmed by the sight of so many blended together. The walls around me were a combination of red and gray, with shots of green and blue swirled in like marble. I reached out to place my hand on the nearest surface, surprised to find it smooth and cold.

"It's glass," Ryland explained, appearing before me. "The walls are made of glass that's been spelled to hold everything I could put here, and to contain any magical blast."

"It's the magical version of a bomb shelter," I mumbled.

She said something else, but I was distracted by everything that surrounded me that I didn't make out the words and didn't care to ask her to repeat herself. Windows perforated the walls, which made no sense. The entire thing was almost translucent to begin with. Why would it need windows?

I took a step toward one, but then caught sight of a portrait that was propped against one of the walls. Changing my course, I circled the comfortable-looking couch and picked up the painting, surprised to see Ryland there. She wasn't alone, though. There were two young girls holding on to her hands. No doubt, her children.

"I painted that." Ryland's voice at my side made me jump. I'd been so engrossed in the details that I hadn't realized she'd approached.

"You have a family," I said dumbly. I didn't know what else to say.

Ryland, the genie, the creature I'd been searching for, wasn't a monster.

She was a *mother*.

"I *had* a family," she corrected. "They've been dead for a long time. Since before I was ever condemned to this bottle, actually."

"That's terrible," I said without thinking.

Ryland sniffled, and I offered her what comfort I could and wrapped my arms around her. I mean, she'd already brought me into her bottle, so giving her a hug wasn't going to kill me.

"Those windows aren't really windows," she told me. "They're all the memories of the time in my mortal life."

"Well, that's just depressing." I moved away from her and got a look at the first window I came to. "Who would do that?"

Ryland's laugh was bitter. "Being a genie is a curse, Charisse. It's not magic, fun, and games. It's torture, meant to be inflicted on someone who was so selfish in their mortal life that they couldn't care less about the feelings or wishes of others. It's only after granting three wishes, real wishes that are meant to change a person's life, that we're given a chance at freedom. By that point, our old life is over, and we have a chance at a fresh slate."

There was so much pain in her words, so much hurt, I couldn't even comprehend what she'd gone through. I'd lost Abram, but my life still went on. Did it hurt more to know your fresh slate could never, ever include the people you loved?

"Is that why you're working with them?" I asked. "Is that why you're taking orders from The Brothers? Are they going to send you back to your human life? To before your family died?"

Ryland met my gaze, and I saw something there. Doubt. In what she was doing, and who she was working for.

She shook her head. "My family died a long time ago, and after it happened, I tried to take my own life. All the power in the world at my fingertips, and I'm useless without there being a wish to activate it."

I stared at her, wondering if our lives were so very different after all. "What happened?"

"I lived in a village, a small little fishing village on the coast. We were happy, for a while. Then, there was war, like always. The soldiers raided our village, killed everyone. My family included." Ryland stared into a window across the room, and I knew it held the memory she was talking about. "I was the only survivor. I couldn't handle it."

I couldn't offer her any more comfort though. There was nothing to say or do that would take away that pain.

"I tried to kill myself," Ryland admitted again. "I threw myself off the cliff outside our village. I was sinking, too, down into the depths of the ocean. While I was there, slowly dying, a bottle that someone had thrown into the sea rubbed up against my body." She waved her arm around, and I knew that we were standing in the bottle that she'd rubbed against. "The rest," she said quietly, "is history. I wasted my wishes on trying to bring my family back, or by trying to go back to before they died. I wasted them, and now I'm stuck cursed."

"Wasted how?"

Ryland pressed her lips together and shook her head, tears springing to her eyes. Whatever it was that had happened with her wishes, she wasn't ready to talk about it.

"You didn't try to pass the curse to anyone like you did Huntsman?" I asked.

I found it really hard to believe she'd just accept her fate and stay in a bottle forever. No one, not even the most self-sacrificing person I knew, would ever do that.

Ryland scoffed. "Are you kidding me? I don't have a life to go back to. I don't have a future. Why would I try to break this curse, to trap someone else in it?"

"But you're encouraging *me* to go back," I pointed out. "You want me to take The Brothers up on their offer to go back to my life before magic. How is any of this relevant to you trying to convince me to take the offer?"

"It's a decision, Charisse. One that only you can make. I wanted you to see that not everyone is given the chance to go back. To make their life better. You have that chance. Don't squander it by doubting the gift you're being offered."

"If you could…if you could go back, and make your life better…would you do it?"

"In a heartbeat," Ryland said. "But not even the most powerful wish could do it. I've tried. Witches and mages have tried. I even called in a favor with an old friend of yours, while she was still alive. But not even Satina was able to do anything about it."

It was heartbreaking, to know the real story behind the genie's life. And I didn't want to know. Honestly, it was easier to think of her as just looking out for herself. Now, I had to consider what she was saying, as well as everything she was able to offer me.

"You don't have time to think," Ryland said. "Not much of it, anyway. The Brothers want an answer. They want this to be over. That's why they sent me."

"I don't like this," I admitted. "I don't like being forced into a corner and being told that there is no way out. It's probably my least favorite thing in the world. All I want to do is tell The Brothers where they can shove it."

"That would be a mistake." Ryland tsked. "The Brothers have everything. They control almost everything they want to. If you think their focus is intense now, it's not. This is only you barely avoiding them. Getting on their nerves. If you turn down the offer now, you're going to bring down the worst that they could do. Not only to you, though. No. They'll destroy everything and everyone that you have *ever* cared about. You think that this, what happened with your friends, is bad? They were just protecting themselves from going down with you. No. If you don't take their offer, everything is going to end."

When she put it like that, even I thought she made sense. It's not like I needed to stay here, not with Ramsey and everyone else already abandoning me. If I could go back, start over, maybe I could make a different decision. After all, hadn't I only gone this way because I didn't have a choice?

"I'll do it," I told her. "I'll take their offer."

With the decision made, I felt the weight of the world shift from my shoulders. At least for a second.

Right up until Abram slipped into my mind.

My love for him, the way I wanted to be with him, still. Even though he wasn't *my* Abram.

As purple smoke filled the bottle, this time I wasn't afraid. I knew the genie was bringing us back to the real world. Once there, I would have to make sure she understood. In that split second, my decision had changed.

My surroundings spun, and my stomach clenched again. Time was running out.

"I've got one condition," I said breathlessly. I could barely hear myself over the howling wind surrounding us. Could she even hear me? "I want to meet with them," I shouted over the wind. "The Brothers have to come to me, in person, to make the deal."

I blinked. That's all I did. We were in the bottle, in the eye of the storm. And with a blink, we were standing in the throne room of her castle, the doors behind us creaking open slowly.

"Oh, my dear," came a familiar but implacable voice. "We've been with you the entire time."

CHAPTER 25

THE VOICE WAS ACHINGLY FAMILIAR, but laced with a staccato that I didn't recognize. I turned with the feeling I wasn't going to like what I was about to see.

Huntsman?

It couldn't be, though. He wasn't dressed the same way. This guy was tall and athletic, with the body of a man who spent hours working outside. He was wearing a pair of designer slacks that hugged his thighs, and a pair of black loafers that went perfectly with his outfit.

I stared at his chest, where a button-down shirt barely fit his muscles, and his sleeves were nocked at the elbows. On his face, there was barely enough stubble for me to call it a beard. His eyes, though. Those were the biggest tell that he wasn't Huntsman. His eyes were the darkest shade of green I'd ever seen. If there wasn't a glint of sun peeking in through the windows on his face, I'd have thought they were black. No, this was not my friend.

"At least you're not stupid as well as naive," he said with a smile. "That's a pleasant surprise. I'm still shocked at how ridiculous modern people are."

He stuck his hands in the pockets of his pants and leaned back against the wall next to Ryland and me.

"Who are you?" I asked, though I didn't need to. Clearly he was like...Huntsman's twin? Or at least brother. The resemblance was eerie.

"My name is Darcus, but you know me as one of The Brothers." He chuckled. "I find that I prefer when people call us The Company, however. It seems so much more professional, don't you think?"

Before I could stop myself, I was taking a step toward him, with my finger lifted and pointed at his face. "You did this. You caused all of this. Everything I've gone through is because of you."

"You know now, just like you've known all along, what happens if you stick that pretty little nose into things that you don't belong in. You still did it, though. Didn't you?" Darcus stared at me with a cocked eyebrow, and the most relaxed stance I'd seen since coming back to New Haven. "Time and again, you stepped into things you shouldn't have. It didn't matter what we threw in your path, or what type of wrench we tossed at you. We even made you think that you were going to lose the man that you loved. What did you do?"

When I didn't answer, he looked pointedly at me, and I flushed under his scrutiny.

"You turned around and spent the next year honing skills that you should never have possessed," he said, shaking his head. "Well, my dear. It's time you gave up those powers and went back to life like the rest of the world."

"Why?"

"I'm not here to discuss the whys and hows with you, Ms. Bellamy." Darcus took a step forward, pulling his hands from his pockets and lacing his fingers together. "I'm here because your condition for accepting our offer was to meet." He shrugged. "I'm here. Now, since you're willing to go back to a time before your power as a Dual was discovered and awakened, it seemed fair to give you a chance to meet me."

"Tell me," I insisted. "Tell me what happens if I go back? Are you going to murder me and take my power?"

Darcus laughed, and for a moment I forgot that I hated everything about him on principle. It didn't stop me from wanting to stomp my foot, though.

"I don't think you understand how this works," Darcus said. "I can't just send you back and take your life like some kind of time-traveling murderer. No. I'm going to strip your Dual nature from you here, and *then* send you back. Take you back to the beginning of your time here in New Haven, and give you the life you should have lived. A Dual." He shook his head emphatically. "You never should have existed."

He couldn't be for real right now. Everything I'd gone through was just because he thought I didn't belong? There had to be more to it than that.

I stared at him, like he was as crazy as he'd come across. "You're telling me that all of this is just because I wasn't 'supposed' to be here?"

"You don't know anything of the magical world. Even after living in it, breathing magic, for how long?" He sneered. "You, Ms. Bellamy, are wasting the power you have."

He was angry now, and I could feel the power coming off him. It was like a tidal wave, gaining power with every inch that it traveled away from his body. By the time it hit me in the chest, I was almost drowning in it. All he did was smile, but that told me that he knew what he was doing to me.

"I'm stronger than you are, Ms. Bellamy. I always will be. You cannot control any of your power, and you're causing all of this. You couldn't save your friends. You couldn't keep them from betraying you. You couldn't even stop New Haven from becoming one of your own personal hells. So you see, I didn't do this. *You* did. Your magic is creating a domino effect, not just here, but all around us. The entire world is being affected because *you* shouldn't exist."

Ryland cowered in on herself, and I got angry. Pissed, really, didn't do this emotion justice. It was rage and fury and hate all rolled into one and pressed tightly into my chest. But the worst part was, he wasn't wrong. I *couldn't* control it. Even now, I was having trouble reining in my desire to lash out.

"You've ruined the status quo," he went on, "and the only thing to do about it now is to remove your power, and for you to take your rightful place."

Char. Ryland's voice echoed in my mind.

I snapped to attention, barely glancing at her. If she was telling me something in my mind, there was reason she wasn't saying it where Darcus could hear.

What's wrong? I tried to seem like I was enraptured in Darcus and his words, but really I was waiting on the genie to tell me whatever it was she planned on telling me.

Not everything is as it seems. Not every sacrifice must be made. Not every betrayal is real. I'm sorry for the part I played, but I had no choice.

Magic exploded from my body at her words. There was no other way to describe it. I couldn't hold it in. I couldn't stop the power as it flashed from my fingertips. Ryland was just another victim of The Brothers. Just another person picked at their weakest and trapped forever.

I was sick of it, and the magic seemed to agree.

Darcus didn't look amused. He was straining under the pressure of the power flowing through my body. It was easily twice what I'd felt from him earlier, and there was no doubt in my mind I didn't have long until he retaliated.

Ryland stared at me, her purple eyes shining with something close to fear and her fake smile looking more like a grimace. I knew, though, what had to be done. She might not want her curse to break, but there was no reason for her to be trapped in a bottle for the rest of eternity. She'd taken the time to tell me about her family, about what she'd lost. The least I could do was let her go.

"Time to go, genie." I didn't mean to sound threatening. I didn't mean to cause the fear on her face to amplify. "Go home and kiss your girls."

Every bit of power I had at my fingertips moved to follow my command, and I knew it had worked when Ryland vanished. Her bottle, the telltale sign of her imprisonment, lay broken on the floor. But I wasn't done yet.

"What did you do?" Darcus snarled. "You freed the genie?" He raised his hands, and his power flared to life.

"I guess it looks that way, huh?" I said, smirking despite myself. Last thing I needed to do was piss him off *more*.

"That's not supposed to be possible!" he roared.

This was it. I had no idea what would happen, or what was coming. But I knew that going back wasn't an option. Not when he was going to take away the one thing that made me special.

"Do you know what you've done?" He grabbed a piece of the bottle. His fingers trembled, and I knew that there was something significant about freeing Ryland. "Do you know how much power, time, and effort went into making sure this went perfectly? It's not easy to stage a betrayal this significant." He was spitting mad, and the red blotches on his face turned a handsome countenance into something horrific.

Those words. Betrayal. My friends…

The doors to the throne room opened behind Darcus, and my mouth fell open as my friends rushed through them. Even Lulu followed the others, looking as though she'd just run a marathon.

"Char!" she cried. "Please don't do it."

"Don't go back." Briar gasped as she leaned down and pressed her hands to her knees. "Genie. Spell."

Even Stacey looked panicked. "Not this path," she said breathlessly. "This isn't a good path."

Ramsey was the only one who looked like he wasn't out of breath. He'd been making me get up early to exercise and run for a year. That entire year, Briar said the only thing she'd run for was food or zombies.

"I can take it all away," Darcus interrupted, suddenly taking up my entire line of sight. "I can take away all the pain that you've gone through. That these people have put you through. All you have to do is take my hand."

He reached for my hand, but I pulled back. There was something wrong, so very wrong, with everything that was going on.

"Just take my hand, Ms. Bellamy. We had a deal."

"Can I have Abram back?" I whispered. "Can you give me the real Abram. Send us back together, without his beast. Give me him, and I'll do it."

"Yes," Darcus insisted. "I can do it. Just take my hand."

"Liar," I said quietly. "You can't break Satina's spell."

I backed away, knowing I had to get away from him. He stepped closer as I retreated, but my magic was there with me. It formed a wall between me and Darcus, keeping me safe from whatever he was trying to do to me. Whatever it was, he had to have my hand for me to go with him. That would never happen. Especially now that I knew he was lying.

"Don't let him touch you," Stacey called.

Darcus turned his snarl on the other woman. "What are you doing here, Teller?"

My hackles went up. "She's my friend, so shut your mouth," I snapped. "Don't even think about going after her."

"We didn't betray you," Briar called from where she stood on the other side of the room. "The genie did it."

Darcus reached for my arm. Thankfully, I'd spent who knows how many years bending my body into strange positions while I was modeling to reach certain poses. Using flexibility I hadn't had a reason to use in years, I bent out of his grasp and rolled away once my body hit the floor. With a burst of speed I hadn't expected, I got away from him.

"This isn't over, Ms. Bellamy." Darcus took a step back. "However, I'll leave you now, since you've seemed to have gained a following."

He was gone in the next instant, and if we weren't all staring at the spot where he'd been, I'd think I was going even crazier than I already was.

"Is it just me," Lulu started, "or does he look just like that Huntsman guy?"

"They have different eyes," I pointed out needlessly. "I thought the same thing. It's like they could be brothers."

I'd thought it before, but I hadn't fully considered it until that moment. As soon as the words were out, though, I knew it was the truth.

"Huntsman," I said desolately. "*No.*"

He stepped through the door, and my worst fear was realized.

"Why would you do this?" I asked. "To me? Was it all a game this whole time?"

Huntsman stood with Abram by his side, and I knew that at least part of what the genie had said was the truth.

"He's your brother," I said, matter-of-fact. Heaven help him if he tried to lie to me now.

"He's my twin," Huntsman admitted. "Please, Charisse. You need to let me explain."

I was already advancing with my hand in the air. I could feel the spell working itself down my arm and into my palm, ready and willing to decimate him with whatever was on hand.

"No," I cried. "No, I *don't* need to let you do *anything!*"

"I tried to stop him." Huntsman held out his hands, palms up. He looked like he was broken, with slumped shoulders, and tears in his eyes. "He can't be stopped, though, not by me. You saw the letter. He's willing to do anything to keep his power. I even got the Tellers involved, so that they could help keep you safe when the time came. The genie, she was his tool...and the Tellers were mine. Stacey was able to help manipulate situations to make sure Abram was here. To make sure that you didn't sacrifice yourself for your friends."

"We knew you'd never sacrifice Abram," Stacey said.

I glared at her, and she shut her mouth immediately. Then, she took a step behind Huntsman for good measure, which might have saved her life.

"I want to know everything," I demanded. "This is your one shot. Spill it. *Now*."

"I will tell you all of it. But we can't do it here." He waved his hands to indicate our surroundings. "You broke the genie's spell, and New Haven is already unstable. We must go."

"I'm not leaving, nor am I taking another step, until you give me Abram back. *My* Abram," I corrected. "I want him back, with *all* of his memories."

Huntsman shook his head, and I felt everything inside me come to a standstill. He was not about to tell me that it wasn't possible. I'd just sent a freaking genie back in time to live her life with her family. He was not going to take Abram away from me.

"Charisse," he said gently. "*You've* had the power the entire time. You're the only one who has the power. You just have to use your blood to make it happen."

"I've never had to use my blood to work magic," I said numbly. "I'm already a Supplicant and a Conduit."

I bit my thumb and held it over my palm, not knowing what I was doing.

"Use your love," Huntsman said, guiding me. "Draw your love in the palm of your hand. Call him back to you."

I put everything I had into that spell. I put my heart, my soul, my mind, and every ounce of the power I had into calling Abram back to me. I put so much energy into it that I couldn't keep my eyes open. Even with my eyes closed, I could feel Huntsman standing next to me. One moment, I was falling to the floor, and the next I was in a strong pair of arms.

"Hunt," I said with the last bit of my strength. "You have so much to explain."

"I know, Charisse," he said soothingly. "First, I'll take you home. Then, I'll tell you the truth about my brother and The Company."

CHAPTER 26

I OPENED my eyes when I heard the familiar sound of people yelling in the distance and cars honking their horns.

"We're back in New York?" I looked around and saw the apartment I'd lived in for the past year, surprised I'd missed the trip from New Haven.

"Yeah," Stacey chirped. "It seems like Hunty here has been hiding a bunch of tricks up his sleeve. Not the least of which is the ability to use small bits of magic. Like teleportation."

"Well." I glared at the man in question. "That would have been nice to know sometime in the past, I dunno, forever." I fumed.

Distracted momentarily by the fact that I felt like someone was driving a train through my head, I remembered what happened right before blacking out.

"Where's Abram?" I sat up and immediately started looking for him before Ramsey pushed me back down onto the couch.

"He's in the guest room," Huntsman said. "He's sleeping. Which is fine, because we have a lot to discuss."

"You're damn right we do," I snapped. "You care to tell us

about how you're one half of the problem we've faced over the last year?" I was beyond angry, that was for sure. "Oh, how about the fact that you stood by and let Satina's father come back to life and take over the body of someone I cared about?"

As everything that had happened came rushing back, suddenly I wasn't in the mood to be very forgiving of the man who'd insinuated himself into my life.

"Charisse," he said stonily. "Not everything is what you think it is."

Gone was the man I'd known, the one who was respectful and out of place in his own skin. Before me stood the rougher version of Darcus. He had more muscle, more intensity, and just *more* than Darcus had. If I had to guess which was the more powerful, it would most definitely be Hunt.

"Wait." I held up a hand, keeping him from saying anything else. "Is Huntsman even your name?"

He looked at me, likely gauging how his response would be taken, before slowly shaking his head.

Ramsey sighed. "You're shitting me."

"My name is Jothi," Hunt said. "But I haven't gone by that since the day I left my brother to the mess he'd created. I walked away from that life."

I walked into the kitchen and grabbed the bottle of vodka that I kept on top of the fridge. I didn't care what time it was —I was going to need alcohol to get through everything going on. Especially if he was going to keep changing what I knew to be the truth.

Not bothering to grab a glass from the cabinet, I brought the whole bottle with me back to the living room.

Stacey was sitting on the couch, so I took a seat next to her and handed her the bottle with a grunt. Her smirk told me that I'd done exactly what she wanted. When she twisted the cap off and took a large drink of it, exhaling deeply after she did so, I knew I'd like her after all.

"Did you know about any of this?" I asked her. "Any of this shit with Huntsman?"

"No," she said. "I mean, I knew that The Brothers have always had something to do with my family. The Company, I guess. But I've never interacted with them. And everything that I've seen or learned about your family, none of it ever indicated that he was anything more than the man you found in Grimault. This line of events… It never went this way or got this far in any version I've seen. But maybe that's a good thing."

I glared at her, and she raised her hands defensively.

"Good," she said, "in the sense that in all the other versions, things don't work out for all of us. So maybe this time they will?"

She handed the vodka to me, and I knew she was telling me the truth. There was something in her voice, in the way she was completely at ease around me, that told me she was good.

"Okay," I said. Then I took the biggest gulp of vodka I could manage, relishing the way it burnt as it slid down my throat.

Turning my glare on Huntsman, who was standing in front of my T.V., I practically snarled at the man. "Start at the beginning and tell me. From the beginning."

Ramsey stood against the wall with his arms crossed. Stacey pulled her legs up and sat with them tucked to her chest. I made myself comfortable, and then all three of us were settled in for Huntsman to tell us his story.

Huntsman shifted, and it seemed like the entire weight of the world fell on his shoulders. He wasn't confident. He wasn't powerful. He wasn't anything except for the man standing in front of me, and it was as though there was a piece of him that was missing.

"My brother, Darcus, was the first of the Conduits. I was the first Supplicant. We were created by the gods, as a way to guarantee they would always have power. With every spell, every transformation, a bit of the power we created would travel to them. It was genius, on their part."

"The gods aren't real," Ramsey interrupted, and I wanted to smack him. Thankfully, Stacey threw a pillow at him for me.

"Shut up," she snapped. "You know nothing."

I snickered as she quoted one of my favorite shows, before remembering that we were in the middle of a very important conversation. My attention shifted back to Hunt, and I waited for him to go on.

"I can assure you that the gods are, in fact, real. They're more powerful than we are. And we're more powerful than anyone else. But our power is divided. That's the way it's always been, until the first and only Dual was prophesied."

He stared at me pointedly, and I took another drink of the vodka I was clutching.

"Darcus went completely insane when he realized what that much power could bring him. He was obsessed with overthrowing the gods. He wanted to prove something, to either them or to the rest of the world. I don't know. Our nature, as Supplicants and Conduits, was intertwined. Every Supplicant had a partner in their Conduit. Darcus, though... He began to teach the other Conduits to use magic that was destroying their Supplicants. We begged them to stop. I begged my brother to stop. He refused, though, and planned an uprising against the gods and their power."

"Holy shit," Stacey murmured next to me. "I've heard bedtime stories that aren't as good as this."

Hunt just kept talking like she hadn't interrupted. "When pleading with him didn't work, I sought the help of a mage. That's how we got away. That's how I ended up in Grimault. The spell was powerful enough to hide them. To hide everyone. And my brother can't very well stage an uprising with only my blood. Plus, he's not powerful enough to take me on by himself."

"That's why he wants Charisse," Ramsey deduced. "He wants her because she was the Dual in the prophecy. He's still trying to overthrow the gods."

"Why?" I asked. "I mean, I get it. He wants power, but *why*? What does he want the power for? There must be some ultimate goal."

Hunt stared into space for a second. "I don't know," he said, confirming my suspicions. "By the time I realized that something was wrong, the bond between us was severed and there was no way for me to discover why he was going crazy."

"Wait," Stacey said suddenly. "I need snacks for this. That's the only way I'm gonna get through this."

I agreed, actually. I didn't know if it was the vodka, or the fact that I didn't remember the last time I'd actually had something to eat that was delicious.

"Great idea," I told her. "Ramsey." I snapped my fingers. "Get us some snacks."

I sat back and pulled the blanket off the back of the couch, then wrapped it around my lap and offered some to Stacey, who smiled and took the offering. While we waited for Ramsey, who was shuffling around in the kitchen, Hunt stood there with defeat written all over his face.

"So," I whispered to Stacey. "You're attracted to one of The Brothers?"

She gasped, slapping me on the shoulder, and her face flamed.

"Oh." I snickered. "You're embarrassed. You, who were shamelessly flirting with him before, you have nothing to say now?"

"That was before I realized that he's one of the most powerful beings in the entire world." She hissed. "Shut up."

"Not a chance," I told her. "When all of this is over, I'm

gonna play matchmaker. Come on, you know it's all sorts of sexy that he's almost as powerful as a freaking god."

Before she could say anything else, Ramsey appeared in front of us with a bowl of popcorn.

"Perfect," I said happily. Then I waved a hand at Hunt, motioning for him to keep telling his story while Stacey and I stuffed our faces on the feast in front of us.

"When I realized we weren't safe," he went on, "I got the Supplicants as far away as I could, and I had them protected. That's how I ended up in Grimault."

He wasn't telling us everything. I bought myself some time to study him while I chewed on an extra large handful of popcorn. Weighing my options, I thought about what I could do. If I forced him to keep talking about it, he might clam up and never share the rest of the details with me. On the other hand, I could let him think I wasn't suspicious, and then pounce when he least expected it.

"Why does he want me?" I asked as a compromise. "Why does he think he wants my power?"

"I don't know." He shrugged. "That's what makes him dangerous. He is already powerful. He already has enough to live forever, and you see the way the supernatural community fear us. He doesn't need any more. But that is what makes him dangerous beyond belief. He is more ferocious than the wolf that hunts in the dead of night, or the monsters that haunt the shadows."

"It was you," Abram said, suddenly appearing in the doorway. "You were the one that got rid of the voices in my head."

My head spun, and I stared at the two men. There was something happening, the undercurrent speaking volumes that they weren't saying aloud. Finally, Hunt nodded.

Abram stepped forward, and I thought he was about to attack. My mouth was open in a warning, but Abram pulled

Hunt into a hug. One that looked just as awkward from the outside as it must be like for the two of them.

But it was also kind of hot.

"You saved my life," Abram told him just loud enough for the rest of us to hear. "I thought I was going to have to kill myself to get rid of the evil he was planning. But you stripped him from my mind. How did you do it?"

He released Hunt, who looked bashful at having attention on him that wasn't all negative. Stacey was looking at him in awe, and more than a little bit of appreciation. Even Ramsey seemed impressed. I, however, was still trying to catch up.

"Holy shit," I said when I finally did. "Satina's father. You're the one who got rid of him. The one who freed the way for the mark. That's how Abram lost his memory."

As angry as I was as Huntsman for keeping things from me, I was more relieved that he'd saved Abram. Part of me could even understand why Huntsman didn't tell me the truth. There were things I had to learn for myself. Decisions I had to make.

"Wait." I paused. "If you're a Supplicant, how did you work magic that powerful?"

He chuckled, and it was the first time I'd ever heard something so carefree coming from him. "Charisse, the power flowing through my veins is so vast that a spell of that magnitude was nothing. It was the same as casting a spell to illuminate the darkness, for a mage. Most Supplicants have those same abilities, but don't realize it. Their magic has been lost over time from years in slavery to the Conduits and then in hiding. But it's possible. Supplicants aren't as weak as the Conduits would have you believe."

He looked at Ramsey, who crossed his arms in front of his chest in a silent challenge.

"The power that *you* have…well, that could do what I did a thousand times over without ever breaking a sweat," Huntsman said. "I simply meant Supplicants aren't as powerless as believed. They simply have to be trained properly in order to access it."

"Hey," Ramsey said. "You try training her. She's impossible."

"He's right." I shrugged, unashamed. "I'm stubborn. But since I'm also a Conduit, it's not really that important to learn my Supplicant abilities, right?"

Huntsman pressed his lips together and raised his eyebrows, but I didn't press for more. I could only handle so much at a time, and I was reaching capacity quick.

My gaze wandered over to Abram, and I caught his eyes locked onto my body. When he glanced up and saw that I knew he was watching, he smiled at me. This wasn't the smile of the impersonator, or the man who'd come to be when he lost his memories. This was *my* Abram, and I knew he remembered everything.

Relief flooded every inch of me, from my scalp down to my toes. The heat in his eyes said much more than words ever could. Especially since we were surrounded by others. I clenched my hands into fists, wanting them all to be gone. To have time with him. But I knew that it would have to wait. We still had answers to get from Huntsman.

"What now?" I turned back to Hunt, who tore his eyes away from Stacey. Oh, they were definitely going to end up together.

"Now, Charisse Bellamy, you prepare for the war that Darcus will undoubtedly bring to your door. And you do so with all of the information, with all of the knowledge, that the fate of the world lies with your ability to defeat him."

"Why the world?" Stacey blushed when everyone turned their attention on her. "I mean, I haven't seen or heard of anything that would indicate that this is an end of the world type of situation. Also, my vision said that someone was going to die. No one died. So things don't always go the way fate originally planned. Just sayin'."

"Ms. Bellamy has a way of breaking things," Abram said with a smile. "She's done it from the moment she tumbled into my life. There's no doubt in my mind that she's gone ahead and broken fate while she was at it."

"I have no choice," Hunt murmured. "Since you turned down the offer to give up your power, I must stay. If you don't learn how to harness your true power, you'll tear the world apart at its seams."

"Oh," I said. There was nothing else to say in response. I didn't realize there had actually been some truth to the things Darcus has been saying.

I'd made the right choice, though. Hadn't I?

I took a deep breath and tried to figure out where to go from here. Thankfully, there was a knock at the door, which was enough to distract Ramsey and the others. He went to check it, while Abram and Hunt had a whispered conversation. I turned to Stacey and struggled to put my thoughts into words.

"You know," she said quietly. "In all the different futures that I've seen, none of this comes to pass. You completely threw me for a loop back there. I thought for sure I'd have to figure out how to travel back in time to find you."

"I'd never leave him," I told her. My eyes stayed on Abram, and she knew what I meant without me saying anything else. "There's nothing I wouldn't do for the people I love," I said. "Oh no!"

Everyone turned to me, but I was already up off the couch and going for my phone. "Lulu! I need to make sure she's okay."

While the phone rang and I waited to hear from her, Abram stepped up to my back. He was so close I could smell him, and I practically melted into his chest. The musky scent that was solely him had my body reacting in ways that it shouldn't in front of company.

"Soon," he growled in my ear as Lulu answered.

"Char." She sounded happy. "How are you doing? Are you still planning on coming to visit next month for Alice and Jack? They miss their Auntie."

I breathed a sigh of relief. Surely if something was wrong, she would have opened with that.

"I'm great." I choked back a sob. "I just wanted to say hey. Yes. I will definitely be there next month."

"Good," she said. "Don't forget to bring Abram. We haven't seen him since that whole crazy weekend in New Haven."

There was dead air after that, and I pulled my phone away to see that she'd hung up on me. Dark chills sparked every inch of my flesh.

Strange. She hadn't once mentioned Abram in the time since the townspeople of New Haven had tried to kill him.

I didn't say anything out loud, but I knew it had to be a side effect of my magic going out of control before. I wasn't going to question it, though.

"She's fine," I said to no one in particular. "Lulu's fine."

I wish I believed me.

"Pizza's here," Ramsey said.

He handed me a box of my favorite and went back to the living room with the rest of the boxes.

"Great," I said. "Pizza and plans to save the world."

Abram slid it out of my hand and set it on the counter.

"The world can go to hell, Ms. Bellamy. You belong to me."

EPILOGUE

ABRAM'S HANDS WERE EVERYWHERE, stroking my body and bringing me right to the edge. Then pulling back just enough to make me moan with the need to have him where he'd abandoned his ministrations.

"More," I demanded. "I need more."

"Say it again." He growled against my neck, biting down when I didn't immediately say the words.

"No." I mewled breathlessly as he teased me again.

"Say it." Abram lowered his head and pulled my nipple into his mouth, causing my back to arch.

"I'm yours." I gasped. "I'm yours."

"Only mine, Ms. Bellamy."

I nodded in acceptance. I was his. Only his. Always. Forever.

"Abram," I pleaded with him. "I need you."

He gave me everything. His heart, his soul, and his hard cock pressed right up against my soaking wet entrance.

"Hold on to me, Char."

I barely had a chance to wrap my legs around his waist before he was thrusting completely inside me.

"Oh, yes!" I screamed as he filled me up.

My body clenched, and I fought the urge to start moving. My body needed a moment to adjust to how fast he'd taken me. I kept still, until I felt him slowly retreat. Instinctively, I clenched my legs around his waist and pulled him back, groaning at how amazing it felt to have him buried inside me.

"Charisse," he warned. "Slow down. I'm not done with you yet."

"I don't care," I snapped at him. "I want this."

"Fine." He leaned down and bit me on the nipple, picking up his pace.

Everything was on fire. Electricity sped through my body where we touched, and I knew that I wouldn't last long. His thrusts, combined with the way he was brushing up against my clit, were enough that I couldn't think straight.

"Don't stop," I said. "God, keep going."

He paused, brushing the hair out of my face that I hadn't realized was there. "I'm not a god, Ms. Bellamy. I'm a beast."

"Whatever, beast," I said with a grin.

The smirk on his face was one he hadn't had before. It was an addition that had come with the memories he'd kept from his life without me.

He wrapped his hand in my hair and pulled my face to his. My body was arched off the bed, almost painfully.

"Look at us," he growled.

My eyes stayed locked on his, until I saw his teeth start to elongate. Something about me always brought out the beast, but the *real* powerful being was the man.

I lowered my eyes, looking at where our bodies were joined.

"Touch yourself, Charisse."

I followed his orders, rubbing my clit while his pace became erratic. I was panting, chest heaving with the exertion. Sweat glistened on his naked chest, but his words were what sent me over the edge.

"While I was gone—" He grunted. "—I thought about

this. I thought about this sex. I dreamt about being wrapped in this heat. You are perfect, Ms. Bellamy. And you're mine, for the rest of your life. You're mine."

I came, my body clenching and exploding at the same time. Wrapped around him, I could feel the way his body tensed, and he followed me over the cliff into bliss.

When I finally became coherent enough to move, Abram was already up off the bed and returning with a towel to clean us up.

"You really are a gentleman," I told him with a smile. "I missed you."

"Charisse." His face turned dark for a second, and something passed over his features that had me worried. It was gone the next moment, though. "No matter where I've gone or what I've done, there was never a part of me that didn't belong to you. Even if I didn't remember you."

"I know."

A knocking on the door distracted him, and he turned quickly to make sure I was covered.

"Who is it?" he said through the closed door.

"You're both needed," Ramsey answered, his voice muffled. "It's important."

"Come, Charisse." Abram held out a hand to me. "Put some clothes on, and let's find out what's so bloody important."

Five minutes later, I was dressed and my hair was swept up into a messy bun on top of my head.

I didn't bother with niceties. Ramsey knew that he was interrupting, and that I'd specifically told him and everyone else that I didn't want to be bothered so I could spend time with Abram.

"What is it?" I asked brusquely.

"We have news," Briar said from my kitchen.

When she saw the shirt I was wearing, one of Abram's, she smiled and shook her head in a knowing way.

I got a glass out of the cupboard and poured myself some water, then turned to see what they had to share. "What's going on?"

"We're pregnant!" Briar squealed.

My mouth was hanging open, and I stared at her. Briar. The woman I never imagined as a mother, was going to have a baby. With Ramsey.

"Oh, you are so screwed." I laughed.

Briar nodded and clapped her hands together. "I know, but I've never been more excited about anything in my entire life."

"I'm so happy for you," I told them. "Honestly. Besides the fact that you're going to have the most spoiled child I've ever met. You're going to be fantastic parents."

"I know." Briar beamed. "Ramsey can just use his magic to make sure our baby is always taken care of." The way she looked at her husband tugged at my heartstrings.

First I gave Briar a hug, then Ramsey. They were going to make adorable parents, and I couldn't wait to see their baby.

"Hey, Ramsey," Briar whispered distractedly. "What is that?"

We all turned to see where she was pointing, and I couldn't believe my eyes. There was a portal opening in the middle of my living room. Blue and white flashing lights, swirling together. The works.

"What the hell?" I took a step forward, but Abram grabbed me by the arm and hauled me behind him.

Ramsey did the same thing to Briar, and she and I shared an annoyed glance while we looked around our men to see what was happening.

A man dressed in all black stepped through the portal. I expected that once he stepped through, the portal would close. But it didn't.

When the man turned to look at me, I saw that he was young and covered in tattoos from where his T-shirt ended all the way down to his wrists. They were brightly colored, but I couldn't get a close enough look to make out the details.

"Why is he holding a broadsword?" Briar whispered, and I looked down at his hands.

She was right. He was carrying a broadsword, and looked like he had just come from the middle of a battle. His blond hair reminded me of someone, but I couldn't place it.

"Oh, thank the gods." He took a step closer, but Abram held up a hand in warning, and Ramsey joined him.

"Who are you?" Abram questioned the young man. "What are you doing here?"

He didn't answer Abram, looking around the room like he was searching for something. His eyes landed on me, and he smiled.

"What's going on?" I stepped closer, ignoring the hand that Abram held out in front of me.

"I did it," he said. "I'm not too late. Come on. We've got to go. Before the portal closes."

"She's not going with you," Abram injerected. "You need to give us the answers we asked of you. What's going on?"

"We don't have time. You can stay here and wait for the war to come in fifteen years. Or you can come now, and stand a chance of saving everyone. There's no time to waste. That portal is going to close in thirty seconds. With or without you. All I can say is that if you don't come now, if you wait fifteen years to join us, you may not arrive in time to save Alice."

"Alice?" Moments after I said the name, my confusion was replaced with dread. "Lulu's daughter?"

"Yes," the young man said. "Alice, Lulu's daughter. And *my* sister."

This couldn't be happening, and yet, it was. Jack had come from the future to collect me for the prophesied war. So much for having a chance to train for battle.

I turned to Abram. "I have to go."

"No, Charisse," he said. "*We* have to go."

We turned back to face the portal. It was already closing. This was it.

Now or never.

The war had arrived.

~

Complete the Series with Book Five, *Fractured by the Beast*.

If you enjoyed this installment of The Conduit Series, *check out April Canavan's* Finding Her Dragons, *Book 1 in her Paranormal Romance Reverse Harem Series,* Omega.

ABOUT THE AUTHORS

ABOUT REBECCA HAMILTON

New York Times bestselling author Rebecca Hamilton writes urban fantasy and paranormal romance for Harlequin, Baste Lübbe, and Evershade. A book addict, registered bone marrow donor, and indian food enthusiast, she often takes to fictional worlds to see what perilous situations her characters will find themselves in next. Represented by Rossano Trentin of TZLA, Rebecca has been published internationally, in three languages: English, German, and Hungarian.

www.rebeccahamilton.com

ABOUT CONNER KRESSLEY

Conner Kressley is a USA TODAY Bestselling Author. He is an avid reader and all around lover of storytelling. He's been obsessed with mythology, magic, and all the things that go bump in the night since he could remember. Also, pizza. But who isn't obsessed with pizza? When he's not writing (or even when he is), Conner can be found in the western Texas watching old movies, geeking out over books (comic and otherwise)

www.connerkressleybooks.weebly.com

www.ingramcontent.com/pod-product-compliance
Lightning Source LLC
Chambersburg PA
CBHW031953240626
47153CB00003B/974